IN GOOD FAITH

*This book is dedicated to the memory of
my dear late friend Georg Slinning, and
to Anne S. Leinum without whose contribution
this book may not have been.*

IN GOOD FAITH

M. W. HAGERUP

First published 2015 by DB Publishing, an imprint of JMD Media Ltd,
Nottingham, United Kingdom.

ISBN 9781780915326

Printed and bound in the UK by Copytech (UK) Ltd Peterborough

I am Alpha and Omega, the first and the last: and,

What thou seest, write in a book

Revelation I; 11

PART I: ARRIVAL

Chapter I

In which we meet our hero, M

The world was young, clean-shaven and full of pleasant surprises. M was on an aeroplane to London, it was the fourth of July 1997 and wine came free in little bottles. He was not particularly used to wine, but ventured to try one with the complimentary lunch people over a certain age can remember. Britain was also young again: it was Cool Britannia, with a new political leadership that promised things could only get better. Next to him was a portly, pinstriped fellow with receding, curly hair, who was obviously far more used to such liquids. He gulped down one miniature bottle after another; at what for M seemed an alarming pace, although he was pleased at the absence of puritan guilt.

Drink no longer water, but use a little wine for thy stomach's sake
and thine often infirmities.
1 Timothy V; 23

As they entered London's airspace, turning the plane first with one side down for people on that side to see, then the other side, Mr Pinstripe pointed to a vast stretch of lights with a small rectangular area.

"That's Wembley stadium," he volunteered. "That's where I live."

He pointed to a mass of lights. It was the first thing he had said to M since take-off, and M wasn't sure if it was the wine, or a sudden pang of sentimental home-longing that had prompted the utterance, but he did like the friendliness of the stranger's personal comment.

M was a twenty-four-year-old man from Norway. He had short, wavy, brown hair; square, horn-rimmed glasses, and was dressed in a grey tweed jacket with elbow patches, and brown corduroy trousers. He was from a little coastal town in this small, coastal country where strangers don't talk to each other unless drunk. He looked at the vast expanse of row after countless row of houses and thought: there must be a place for me too, somewhere.

For we are his workmanship, created in Christ Jesus unto good
works, which God hath before ordained
that we should walk in them.
EPHESIANS II; 10

M was on his way to London to be a part of a Christian church, a movement, a revival that was going on in the charismatic Chelsea Chapel. He was a devoutly religious young man, and as the millions of lights passed silently outside the little window M was casting his mind back ten years, to the vision he'd had as a fourteen-year-old boy. His older sister by sixteen years had become involved with Pentecostal Christians in between her wine and pill abuses and kept dragging young, rebellious, long-haired M along to meetings of all sorts. M had always had a fascination with the mystic and the magic, like many kids. Unlike most kids, he had together with a friend, created a cartoon depicting the vampire Count Dracula, and by the early teens he was drawn to pseudo-Satanist heavy-metal groups; highly image-conscious entertainers pretending to be rebellious. Black books and Crawley-literature were absorbed, and a Satan-worship altar constructed in his bedroom, complete with upside-down crosses made from leftover chicken bones from the Sunday dinner, much to his mother's silently anxious disapproval. He could not help wanting to lift the drapes of the world to peep behind and find something, or perhaps not find something. Was it the looking or the prospect of discovery that drove him? Was it just the aesthetics of mysticism, the theatrical aspect of Satanism? He didn't know.

He remembered being taken along to a revival camp-meeting, held in what looked like a big circus tent, with rows of wooden chairs and a stage where the electric worship-band was leading the worshippers in upbeat, trance-inducing music, the electric guitar equipped bandleader announced through the speakers that the next song would make Satan run out of the tent. As soon as the song started, M rose demonstrably and marched out, making sure people noticed him. The theatricality of it appealed to him. He felt in control, directing the 'mise en scène', taking centre stage. And having been taken to a number of meetings, certain words and concepts, and Bible histories crept down into the deep sub-conscious mind of young, impressionable M. So, one grey Sunday, his sister was attending a service at the Happy Life Revival Centre. She'd asked her father to pick her up, and he took M with him to run up and fetch her. M made sure to wear one of his heavy metal, Satanist T-shirts, and once inside it was noticed by one of the young visiting preacher from the Chelsea Chapel, London. He asked M smiling, pointing to the satanic image on the T-shirt, "Do you believe in Satan?"

"Not really," M lied.

After a long discussion on God and Satan, and life and death, M agreed to be prayed for, only – as he thought to himself – to prove that prayer could change nothing and nobody.

A few days later, the subconscious mind did its work, and the accumulation of years of fascination with the occult and mystic, combined with the onslaught of Christian theology of recent months – possibly combined with a heavy meal before going to bed – culminated in a religious vision. M lay in bed and suddenly became aware of a sight before him. There was Jesus on the one side, and Satan on the other. Neither of them said anything. Jesus looked like he does in the western imagery of the Nazarene, and Satan looked like the grinning puppet master that heavy metal rock bands portray him as. Suddenly, the realisation that Satan was evil, and that he wanted the worst possible outcome for us in this world and eternal suffering in the afterlife, and that God was our loving father and wanted only the best for us in this life and heaven forever after; that Jesus was indeed the victor in the age-old struggle between evil and good; that *He* was the strongest, the best, indeed the coolest, became overwhelmingly clear to the teenage M. There and then he chose Jesus Christ of Nazareth as his Lord and Saviour.

if thou shalt confess with thy mouth the Lord Jesus, and shalt
believe in thine heart that God hath raised him from the dead, thou
shalt be saved.
For with the heart man believeth unto righteousness; and with the
mouth confession is made unto salvation.
ROMANS X; 9 – 10

For a fourteen-year-old boy in a non-religious family, in a largely secular society, known among his friends and school mates as a Satanist rebel, choosing to stand up for Jesus wasn't all easy. But M revelled in being contrary to expectations. He carefully nurtured the image of one who didn't care what others said or thought, but more than that: he really felt he was changing into another person. He had something to stand for that was uniquely his, and even if it was M 'contra mundum', all the better for it. It was his Stockman moment, defining him as an eccentric individualist who was "crazy about Jesus". He had a certain reluctant acceptance from his mates, mostly on the basis that he was very good at drawing caricatures of fellow pupils and teachers. Whoever can mock the teachers, and ridicule fellows will more readily be admired. He had his insecurities – feeling less clever because he couldn't stand maths, and feeling his family was less rich than the others because his father never spent money, and feeling less heterosexual because his attractions went both way.

These were, however, offset by M's forceful personality and air of absolute entitlement to undeserved admiration – a result perhaps of a dotingly loving mother – which insulated him from slights and put-downs on account of his belief. He commanded a certain respect, despite his strangeness. But having defined himself as a follower of Jesus, he could only delve deeper into it, which took him away from the social circles of his peers, and into the parallel universe that is the charismatic Christian movement. After a decade he had become the leader of the choir, a member of the board and the organiser of countless events. He was the natural choice when representing the church in the community, a role not diminished when elected to the board of a local political party. At twenty-four he had reached the point where the little church in the little home town provided but very small opportunities to grow in the work of the Lord. M knew there was only one thing for it: London was calling.

Through friends, a room had been arranged for him with the fellow believer Zelma Hernandez. Zelma was a little lady, of indeterminable age, probably around forty, with big, eighties style hair. She was originally from Bolivia, and spoke in a strongly accented Hispanic-English through clenched teeth. By hard work and many sacrifices she had managed to buy her council flat just outside Putney, south London, and was fiercely proud of this. In order to keep afloat financially she took in lodgers in her one bedroom domicile. M, being male, had to sleep on a bed in the living room. The bed doubled as a sofa in the daytime, so he had to make sure to make it nicely in the morning, covering it with a heavy, scratchy blanket Zelma had provided.

M took the first few days to play the tourist and get to know this – for him – new part of London. He had been nineteen years old the first time he ascended the stairs from Piccadilly Circus underground station together with his friend Georg. As he had surfaced from the dark and dank bellies of London his eyes adjusting to the light of day, those mythical buildings took shape before him and all around him the metropolis arose as an urban fairy-tale landscape. This is it. The London of Dickens, of Sherlock Holmes, of Bertie Wooster, and now of M and his jolly chum. He was treading holy ground, and had it not been for the dirt he would have kissed it. M and Georg were not only visiting the city though. Together with 14,998 other believers they convocated on the Earls Court Arena for the week-long Mission To Europe, led by the American evangelist Jacob Cherubo. The two friends would return every year to hear the Word of God, and to inhale and imbibe the drug that is London.

Putney though, was a new discovery for M. He wondered as he wandered through the High Street, looking at trousers, radios, clocks, books and people. It all seemed cheaper and dirtier than Norway, and M liked it. He discovered Marks & Spencer's and was impressed that they had an entire shop dedicated to selling clothes for the elderly. He would later discover it was where normal people could get normal clothes at normal prices. Eventually he came upon what for him seemed a rather large supermarket where the shop workers were dressed in a ghastly brown uniform.

"Poor devils, having to walk around all day in that", thought M.

He had himself worked in a supermarket once, and all that had been required of him was to put on a blue coat with the company's logo. That had been bad enough, but this uniform's drabness took the prize. M wanted to get some supplies and to cook dinner for his landlady that evening. Walking around looking at the prices of things, he was amazed at how much cheaper everything was than Norway. Many things were half the price, some even less. The basket was quickly filled with fruit, bacon, beef, potato, butter and a pudding of some sort. Must have vanilla cream with the pudding, thought M. After circling the dessert shelf a couple of times with no luck, he asked a young brown-clad man where he might find the vanilla cream. A very empty stare was the reply.

"Er, just a moment sir", said the young man and fetched reinforcements in a matronly lady with permed hair.

"Can *oi* 'elp you sir?"

"I am sure you can. I was looking for vanilla cream", replied M.

"Vanilla cream?" she said slowly, as if he'd asked for an illegal substance.

"Yes, I'd like to have it with these puddings". He motioned to the puddings in his basket.

The matron's eyes lit up. "Aow! You mean *custard*!"

"Custard?" M's thought of General Custer, and had no idea what she was on about, but agreed to be shown this mysterious sample of the strange, new world.

The matron conscientiously showed him both the ready-made tinned stuff, and the powder in a bag for genuine home cooking.

"I'll just have the tin and try it", said M, and gratefully put it into his basket.

"Anythin' else oi can 'elp you wit sir?" enquired the matron.

"Er, no, I think that was all", replied M, and went to pay.

With four brimming shopping bags he jumped on the bus back to the flat, and got in just before Zelma came home. He heard her opening the front door as he was unpacking the bags.

"Oh hello Zelma! I've done some shopping," called M from the kitchen as she entered the tiny hall.

"I thought I could cook dinner tonight."

"Ooh, zat eez vunderfool", replied Zelma in her unique accent.

"I found this shop where everything was just *so* cheap, I couldn't believe it", cried M enthusiastically, still unpacking.

Zelma entered the kitchen and looked at the shopping bags. She stopped, transfixed. This was a lady who used a broom and dust tray instead of an electrical, power-consuming hoover; she washed her clothes in the bathtub rather than installing a costly washing machine. Here was an immigrant who, by extreme thrift and hard work, had been able to buy that little council flat and become one of Mrs Thatcher's army of property owning self-improvers. Now, with eyes wide open and jaw hanging she stared as had it been the scene of a heinous crime, which in her eyes it probably had.

"You, you", she began, "you have been to the most expensive zupermarket in all dee country! Why you go to *Waitrose*? I can tell you way to Azda! Eez not far, you take dee buz. And *you* go to *Waitrose*! HA-HA!"

She clapped her hands in a funny sort of foreign sarcastic way that M only half understood, but understood enough to feel foolish.

He cooked the meal, including his speciality; homemade souse Béarnaise, and served the puddings with the mysterious yellow cream, all of which Zelma ate amazingly fast, without any outward signs of appreciation. She gave instructions how to get to 'Azda' and went to bed. M set looking at the dirty dishes feeling depleted and slightly depressed. He peered out at the dark housing estate. There were spots of lights from windows, and he heard voices shouting. Someone was playing the piano – not very well. This was Putney, not London. No view to Big Ben or Tower Bridge from these windows. He wasn't a stone's throw from the British Museum, or a short walk from St James' Park.

But he was here. If New York was the city that never slept, London was the city that had the occasional kip and woke up younger than it had been when it fell asleep. He would make it. Not sure what 'it' was, but he would make something; of that he was certain.

The Lord shall command the blessing upon thee in thy
storehouses, and in all that thou settest thine hand unto; and he
shall bless thee in the land which the Lord thy God giveth thee.
Deuteronomy XXVIII; 8

The next morning he was awoken by Zelma trudging into his bedroom – which was of course her living room – with the local free newspaper. She sat down at the little dining table that stood at the other end of the room from the bed and proceeded to read, or rather hunt, through the newspaper looking for special offers, vouchers, and opportunities for making extra money. She did not say anything. Not 'good morning' or 'hello, time to rise and shine it's a beautiful day,' or any such phrases that one might expect. She just sat there looking fierce and determined. Indeed she didn't have to say anything because her whole being and the fact she was doing something she believed to be a useful thing conveyed the message clear enough to M; it was time to get up and do something useful, not just laze about in bed. M cursed himself for not having brought any pyjamas. Not only because he needed the loo, but also because instead of a duvet he only had that old, coarse, woolly blanket that scratched the skin and provided very little protection from the cold night air that seeped through the single glazed windows and un-insulated walls. After a while of this passive-aggressive non-verbal communication, Zelma stood up and went out. M hurried to the loo and relieved himself, then crept back under the sandpaper-rug and fell asleep.

He awoke as the mid-morning sun finally entered the room and warmed it and him. He made some toast with jam and a mug of tea and sat down on the tiny balcony overlooking the central court of the estate. The grass looked greener, the sky bluer and he felt warm and light.

CHAPTER II

In which our hero applies for a job and attends worship
at the Chelsea Chapel

He had been told that, just like in Norway, there was a public job centre, and that he needed to find his local one and register. He was only looking for a part-time job, to combine with studying applied theology at the London Metropolitan Bible College, which was run by the Chelsea Chapel. The young missionary who had prayed with M for his salvation had come from this church, and Happy Life had maintained a close relationship with it, contributing to M's decision to study there. A decision that was the culmination of a rededication of his life in the service of the Lord, which had happed during his stint in the army. As previously described M had become zealously enthusiastic about Jesus at fourteen, and at this tender young age it had been great fun. The ultra-charismatic church his sister had pulled him along to was a fairly new creation, set up by the former hippie Sigmund Fjeld, his wife Gerd, and a diverse group of new-religious revivalists and sentimentalists. This group challenged the traditional churches in the small, coastal town, and drew unto them a motley crew of disaffected believers and young seekers. Some of these were former – or in some cases *not* so former – drug addicts and petty criminals, finding a new high in the ecstatic, noisy and utterly uninhibited worship at the Happy Life Revival Centre.

The band of long-haired, denim-clad brothers and sisters was the most unlikely of religious groups, and a fascinatingly *non*-conformist heap for the helplessly bourgeois M. Worship was by means of an electric band worthy of the young Led Zeppelin in volume and fuzziness, with a 15-part drum kit and a bass-player as stick thin as his electric instrument. Some would sit smoking at the back of the room; others would be closing their eyes, dancing Woodstock-style, yet others would threaten the devil in aggressive tongues. In between them all, some unwashed children and a big, black, slightly deranged black Labrador called Nero (!) would run freely. It was a cacophony of voices and sounds with only one common denominator: everybody was crazy about Jesus and nobody would in their wildest dreams admit to being 'religious'. They would have prayer-meetings that lasted from nine o'clock on a Friday evening right through the night, then go out on the streets the next day to preach about Jesus, but *against* religion. *Religion was the enemy.* It was the work of the Devil.

Woe unto you, scribes and Pharisees, hypocrites! For ye are like
unto whited sepulchres, which indeed appear beautiful outward,
but are within full of dead men's bones, and of all uncleanness.
Even so ye also outwardly appear righteous unto men, but within
ye are full of hypocrisy and iniquity.
Matthew XXIII; 27–28

This was the fundamental paradigm on which Happy Life Revival Centre's understanding of faith was built: there was a relationship with God and nothing more – it was Lutheranism on speed. Established, formalised worship was the work of men whose initial love of the Lord had turned stale and sour.

The congregation of Happy Life believed in the downfall of the state-church – seen by them all as a hindrance to the revival of Norway; and of the Catholic Church – seen as a hindrance to worldwide revival. It was a happy and exciting time for M and his young friends, as they travelled together to concerts and meetings, played guitar around the campfire and felt part of something big and important. But the imminent revival, the throng of thousands they all waited for impatiently to be harvested for heaven, did not materialise. Instead Happy Life developed its own sacraments and procedures. People started falling away from the narrow, if bumpy path. Some went back to previous sins of drugs, alcohol and enjoyable sex, others crept back to the comfort zones of established churches, one or two were lured away by Mormons and some simply floated about in the fringes. The Happy Life Church became more sanitized, with families, structured worship and a leadership with the power to assert their uneducated egos. Some of Sigmund's original co-founders of the group went away, whilst Sigmund remained to take the reins of pastorship.

M remained also, but unfortunately grew up. M's curse was his intellectual curiosity; he could not help thinking and reading. So after quickly tiring of the religious books on offer in the church, he started delving into the history of philosophy, into psychoanalysis, into ethics and politics. He read Kafka, Dostoyevsky and Ayn Rand. He met the ideas of Aristotle, Aquinas, Descartes, Hobbes, Locke and Kant. He struggled through *The Wealth of Nations* and *Das Kapital*. Pennies dropped in quick succession. He had to acknowledge that he was indeed religious – only a particular *kind* of religious, which is what they had been all the time at Happy Life Church. Nonconformism was not such a new thing and the question of proving God's existence had been dealt with; inconclusively. Revelation was unsure knowledge, if knowledge at all. Even empirical knowledge is uncertain, how could he claim the world was created in seven days, or the virgin birth was fact? And miracles, there were many claims to them, but M had never seen one, and neither had his friends, if they were honest. So, although he still believed in God he drifted. One particular scripture acted as the guy rope to keep his faith's wobbly structure from falling apart:

For now we see through a glass, darkly, but then face to face: now I know in part; but then shall I know even as also I am known.
1 CORINTHIANS XIV; 12

The substance of this being what philosophers have discussed at great length through the ages: that human perception and knowledge is limited. This, combined with the very real sense of revelation his experience at fourteen had left in him, made him choose faith over mere reason. One needn't reject reason altogether, but one should humbly acknowledge that human understanding is only in bits and parts, that we do not possess all the facts, that we have not the instant comprehensive comprehension of an all-knowing Aquinas type God. A God who is boundless and who one day will reveal to us the whole truth, and at that point we 'shall know'.

Seeing the world through this prism, M could find a peace of sorts. It was a strict dualism: science said evolution over million of years was the most likely explanation, God's word said six days. M believed both. And one day, he thought, God would reconcile the seeming contradiction; 'now I know in part'. As he saw it, science was the way in which men struggled to uncover the secrets of nature whilst faith was about discovering truth. If science's conclusions so far did not tally with Gods' revealed Word it was partly because science had not progressed enough, but also partly because it was concerned with *Fact* not *Truth*. Rejecting science would have been beyond the pale for M, but as the in-house religious philosopher he could stay with the little family of church friends that he had established such strong bonds with. One thing is what you believe in, quite another is with whom you take tea; and his friend Georg made very nice tea indeed.

of making many
books there is no end; and much study is a weariness of the flesh.
ECCLESIASTES XII; 12

Then M went off to the army. In Norway they still practiced forced conscription, and although it offended M's libertarian principles, he had to accept it when his application for civilian service on religious grounds was turned down. It was there, among his fellow young men, that he noticed a fundamental difference in his outlook on life, the world, and all things therein. His roommates were quick to stick up pictures of scantily clad ladies – apart from one lad from the countryside who put up pictures of American lorries and tractors. M had no pictures. So the question was eventually popped, like a little balloon filled with the smelly air of suspicion: was M gay, as he didn't have any pictures of sexy dames? M felt it was not so much aversion against a little fruity perversion, which he feared might be much welcomed in the all-male dormitories, but rather the fear of the *non-conformist*. Had he put up pictures of strapping lads with bared torsos they'd probably been more at ease than with M's monk-like scarcity. After all, the tractor guy was never questioned. But M had simply too strong a compulsion, too deeply a felt antipathy against indulging the desires of mortal flesh to ever want to surround himself with imagery to arouse it. And besides he would've felt embarrassed. Should he perhaps have hung some Russian icons by his bed, of the sort he had seen in one of his favourite films, *Andrej Rublev*? And there it is: a three hour long black and white film about a medieval icon-painter, almost without dialogue, and what little there is, in Russian. M was different, and it showed.

M decided to make use of the time in the army and enrolled in a university lecture course on the history of philosophy, science and applied logic, held at the camp by a young lecturer from the University of Oslo. And when the field priest offered lessons in ancient Greek he enrolled for that too. These intellectual activities had him pegged as the intellecto-geek, and with that image he was left alone. He looked at the vacant faces of other young soldiers. He knew he did not belong with them. He longed back to Georg's lapsang souchong tea, the new band he had formed, watching Russian and Polish films into the early hours of the morning, eating cranberry ice cream, and serving God somehow. As he sat through the Greek lessons, he looked at the priest; a youngish High Church oriented Lutheran. He listened to his thin vowels, his soft voice, and realised that this weak, feminised man was doing more for God than he was himself. It had to change. In a private conversation M mentioned he had tried to get out of the conscription on the basis of religious conscience. The field priest was quick to take the hint, and immediately pulled the necessary strings for M to be released. Soon after, M found himself on the train back to his hometown. There had to be a reason for this strange sequence of events. He knew God had put something in his heart. An impatient longing for London. Why? M had always liked England and all things English. He assumed that it was God who had put it there all along.

God; who hath saved us, and called us with a holy calling, not according
to our works, but according to his own purpose and grace, which
was given us in Christ Jesus
before the world began
THE SECOND EPISTLE OF PAUL THE APOSTLE TO TIMOTHY I; 9

After transferring to civilian service, he started putting his things in order. His entire collection of rare art-house films was given to Georg, he sold some things and raised enough cash to buy the ticket and have a little pocket money. At the local jobcentre he requested all the necessary paperwork to claim the Norwegian jobseekers' allowance in Britain. A man in a purple turtleneck jumper and brown sandals with socks told him that he did not recommend going to London to look for work. The unemployment-rate was higher in Britain than in Norway. M looked at this man. He stared into his eyes and saw the abyss of a human being devoid of any sense of adventure. He saw a man straightjacketed by Social Democratic sensibility; one should only go where the national rate of unemployment was slightly lower. Had he not seen the thousands of advertisements for jobs vacant at any one time in the big city? The rate of unemployment might be higher in Britain, but there was still more jobs to be had in London that in the entire country of Norway.

Follow the statistical rate of employment? That was the sensible thing to do. One needed no imagination. Just follow the official state data. Do what everybody else does. Be grateful and careful and afraid.

"I... I, thought I could try at least. I can claim three months of my jobseeker's allowance in any European country".

This very sensible consideration made the turtle necked sandal wearer relent. He prepared the paperwork and then admonished M to buy a return ticket. M was going to do that anyway; it was cheaper than one way. He came out from the jobcentre and shook the Social Democratic dust of his shoes.

And whosoever shall not receive you, nor hear your words, when
ye depart out of that house or city, shake off the dust of your feet.
MATTHEW X; 12–14

M's pastor Sigmund and his wife Gerd had two months previously taken up a pastorship of one of the many 'satellite' churches affiliated with Chelsea

Chapel. All across inner and greater London's suburbs small and medium sized community churches met and were networked together in a sort of corporative religious entity called the London Metropolitan Church, with the parent church Chelsea Chapel as the 'mama-spider' at the centre of the web. Pastor Sigmund had long felt that the little town on the west coast of the little country of Norway had grown far too small for him. He had great plans for, and a great vision of, an international ministry – evidenced by having been on a trip to Africa and another to South-America – and had therefore sought a placement with the London Metropolitan Church. A vacancy arose in Uxbridge, where a small church consisting mostly of pensioners, able to pay a decent salary and provide a car, needed a pastor. Sigmund, who felt the need for a decent salary and a car, accepted the post after some negotiation. For M it seemed as if the voice of God had spoken in all but an audible way telling him to follow suit. He applied for the Practical Theology course at the London Metropolitan Bible Institute, and prepared to immerse himself in the great work that God was doing there.

So here he was, going down an English street, into an English jobcentre with jobs paying very English salaries.

"Hello, M isn't it?" said a fat, bald, and very polite man.

"Yes, that's right" replied M.

They sat down on either side of a desk, and the man started tapping on his dirty keyboard.

Unlike the Norwegian jobcentre this was not a new building, it was not newly refurbished with 'Ikeaish' birch-wood furniture and light colours, the floors were not covered in sensible linoleum but a grey-brown carpet. It was stuffy, overfilled, smelly and felt slightly dirty. Where the Norwegian office was large, cold and almost empty, with two clients for every ten employees, this was close, hot, full of people, bustle, with ten clients for every two employees. It was far better than the Norwegian one, thought M.

M presented his paperwork upon request and the man perused it.

"Roit, so you've brought this form from Norway 'ave you?"

"Yes"

"Roit." He looked at the form entitling M to what was in Norway a medium to low level of jobseeker's allowance.

The fat man tapped with his sausage-roll fingers on the grubby keyboard again, and finally printed out some papers. He got up from a perilously small chair that M thought might collapse any minute under the strain, as it squeaked and groaned. The man came back with the papers and continued to disregard the welfare of the chair. He stared at the documents.

"Blimey! Oi 'ave never seen anyone ge'ing *that* much paid out on jobseeker's allowance before!" He looked up, half admiring M for being from such a generous Welfare State.

"Well, the prices are a lot higher…" M tried, but the man wasn't listening.

He went on to tell M all sorts of things he didn't want to know about the British welfare system. Finally, when all had been said and what little needed doing, done, M was duly entered to the system, with his work experience so far, education and his preferences as to type of work and salary level etcetera, he thanked the man and got up to leave. On his way out he had a look at the board where new jobs were posted on little index cards. He looked under 'part-time' and noticed a vacancy at *The Crest Dairy* requiring a part-time assistant at their milk-bottle depot, night shifts, and with a name and telephone number to contact. What could be more English than to work at a milk-bottle depot thought M? Probably in breach of the rules and regulations, he tore the note down quickly before anyone saw it, and went over to the telephones provided for the use of the job seeking public. He spoke to a man called Ray, and was to come down there at 3pm. The hot, stuffy July air outside felt fresh and reinvigorating, as M emerged from the claustrophobia of the client-state officedom, with a prospect of milk bottle filling in his hand.

For even when we were with you, this we commanded you, that if
any would not work, neither should he eat.
2 THESSALONIANS III; 10

After lunch – which had consisted of one of those curious triangular sandwiches in a little plastic box – M managed to find the right bus and then walked the remaining two to three hundred yards to the dairy. As he neared the large metal gates he felt strangely out of place. It was not the sort of area, nor the sort of job he had imagined himself in. But he would take any job rather than rely on the allowance, and start even on the lowest rung of the employment ladder. With the ominous looking gates behind him he saw a little building with the words 'office' printed on a tatty looking sign. He knocked on the door and a gruff voice told him to come in. M entered and met with the second fat, bald man in a day. But where the jobcentre man was soft and pasty, this man was compact and hard, dressed in a checked shirt and worn jeans. M reckoned he was in his fifties.

"Aow, 'ello Mr M, 'ave yourself a seat, mate".

He gestured to a dirty looking chair covered in black imitation leather.

"Thank you," M said in an over-polite job interview manner, before seating himself carefully down.

"Aw right, tell me a little 'bout yourself," Ray demanded.

M complied and tried to emphasise the importance of a week spent on a fishing-trawler in Norway, a job he'd only been given because his father was the owner's cousin. The career was cut off in its infancy when the boat was impounded by the Coast Guard for fishing with illegally small openings in the nets. The boat had to be turned back to the quayside and M who did not think the work, the cramped conditions, the uneducated crew, the old gay cook, the isolation from the world, the cold, wet, fish, and all the other un-charming elements of the fisheries were worth the generous payment, jumped off after having done his share of the required cleaning of the vessel.

"You can't jump off now, the trip isn't over," a fellow fisherman protested.

"You just watch me," replied M in conscious self-dramatisation.

M didn't feel the need to fill in all these details; it was enough to mention the job experience, as it afforded valuable macho-proletarian credentials. He also mentioned working at the grocery store. The hard ball of a man sat listening; leaning back in his chair, armed folded and rubbing his stubby chin. After a very little while M ran out of things to say and a quick silence fell. The hard man looked at M, smiled and said:

"There's no doubt you're qualified, and I'm sure you could do the job".

M felt a little warm feeling spreading in his chest, tinged only by the expectance of a 'but' hanging in the air.

"But, I ain't gonna give you the job, my man". M's tummy chilled.

"Oh" said M. Too polite to question the hard man's judgment.

"This is where you ask 'why?'" said the hard man smiling.

"Oh yes… er… why?"

Ray leaned forward. "I can tell by the way you speak that you're an educated fellow. I'm gonna get applications from chaps with no education, and kids to feed. You can go out there and get a much better job, any job; they can't".

The practical, no-nonsense, discriminatory wisdom of the judgment presented in this straightforward and strangely caring manner, struck M as both fair and true.

"Yes, I, I can understand that".

"I'm sorry mate but…" said the man, as if resting his case on the self-evident nature of what had been said.

They shook hands, and M wandered off, light and relieved that he didn't have to work at the dairy.

Sunday came and M travelled with Zelma in silence to the Chelsea Chapel, which, as the name implies is situated in the respectable London area of Chelsea. M tried to keep up with Zelma as she burrowed her way through the crowds with the speed and precision of a badger on amphetamines. M soon began to fall behind as he lifted his face, and his eyes began to drink in the well of new impressions. He had been here before, but now he was here *proper*. He wouldn't be returning to Norway in a few days, he was *here*! He felt the ground keenly for every step. He saw the shops, the cafés and the trees. He saw the buses, taxis and mopeds. He saw the blacks, browns and whites. He felt as if he had come out the other side of a looking glass into an utterly different reality to that of his little, Norwegian hometown. The first time M had seen a black person in the flesh he was fifteen. He'd had a Lebanese friend growing up, he'd met a couple of Pakistanis who started up a karate-club, and of course the town had a Chinese restaurant; but apart from one sight in the street when he was a teenager, he had never met a proper, African descended *Negro* (as his mother innocently called anyone with a slightly darker skin-tone than the pale Norwegians), until he met the people from the Chelsea Chapel. His parents had two stock reactions that they always made whenever black people appeared on the telly: his mother would say, "ooh look at their teeth. The Negroes have such wonderful white teeth", and his father would say, "The Negroes are very musical".

M's father's unfulfilled childhood dream had been to learn to play the trumpet like Louis Armstrong. Instead he started work at fourteen and built up his own business, which was doing very well by the time M was born.

The father had grown up in a small village in the country, at a post-war time of scarcity and real austerity. Apart from an unlimited supply of open spaces and fresh air there was little by way of luxury in the eleven children strong household. They had a tiny farm, did some fishing, and M's grandfather was also the village cobbler and handyman. The father would speak respectfully and gratefully about his parents; but seldom with any tender lovingness. Most of his childhood stories were about him asserting himself and standing up to his siblings or other boys, fighting, struggling, but ultimately winning. M's father didn't say much about his childhood Christmases, but what little he did divulge, betrayed a scarcity of presents and material treats that went some way to explain the lavish Christmases he had always ensured were celebrated in *his* household.

His first child, M's older sister, had had so many presents when she was a little girl she fell asleep amid a sea of wrapping paper, with many packets still left untouched. For M the memories of his childhood Christmases were the magical wonders of food, smells, toys and goodies; the unbridled otherness of a transformed world. All the things his father had wanted, he ensured his children had bountifully. And M's mother played her role – the 1950s style housewife – to perfection. For her the children were god, with her husband a close second and herself relegated somewhere further down the order of things, as simply the means to the end. M being the youngest, 16 and 11 years junior his sister and brother respectively, he enjoyed being spoiled even more than a lonely child. He never had to share his toys, and was adored not only by his adoring mother, but by two elder siblings who, when they started earning money, came bearing gifts as well. And as these older ones flew the nest M spent many childhood evenings with his parents, in front of the telly, drinking cocoa and eating waffles served up by his mother. And it was on evenings such as these that the occasional black person would appear, more often than not singing, like Sammy Davis jnr., or playing the trumpet, like Louis Armstrong. And if the issue of black segregation in the southern states of the USA came up his father would always say: "the Americans brought them there by force, so they can't complain about them being there now!"

M supposed it was his father's way of justifying his dislike for the Pakistani presence in Norway. After all they had not been forced to come and they claimed welfare state entitlements, and they were Muslims! M's father, although both intelligent and informed, was completely, consistently prejudiced. Europe was the best part of the world, Norway the best part of Europe, his town the best part of Norway, his street the best part of town, his family the best part of the street, and *he* the best part of his family. This was never uttered as opinions or matters of personal preference, but as matters of objective fact, which could only be disputed by mere idiots. The outlook gave him considerable security in his worldview, but did also somewhat limit his openness to new impulses; including impulses from those whom the Norwegian King Olav had called *'our new countrymen'*. M's father didn't care too much for the foreigners, nor fancy foreign food such as pizza.

"Not proper food" he declared.

Although he could admire individual foreigners who had come and integrated themselves and achieved something or other – he admired the Chinese, saying, "they work hard and don't make any trouble" – he did not care for them as a class. It was therefore difficult for him to grasp that M wanted to leave this picture-perfect small town in the utopian welfare state to make himself a foreigner in an enormous city choke full of other foreigners. Yet that was what his own son had done. M kindly put it to him that when *he* had been a young man he had travelled at sea and 'seen the world'. Now it was M's turn to get out there and see some of the realities of the planet. And what better place to go to than London, into which the whole world comes, thus reducing the travelling required? Framed in this way, M's father had managed to fit M's choices into his cognitive machinery and been reassured that, given time, M not being an idiot, he would necessarily come to the very same conclusions on everything as he had.

Honour thy father and thy mother, as the Lord thy God hath
commanded thee; that thy days may be prolonged, and that it may
go well with thee, in the land which the Lord thy God giveth thee.
Deuteronomy V; 16

M looked around and saw the multitudes of colours and shapes. Many of these different looking people had probably been born in this country, yet if anyone had been asked to pick the foreigner they would not be likely to point the finger at M. He was part of the minority that looked and dressed as an Englishman. But if he had found London full of 'foreigners', it could not have prepared him for the onslaught of multiculturalism at the Chelsea Chapel. The building had once been a chapel, and from under the foliage of surrounding trees emerged a gothic vision of dark grey crumbling stone and masonry. Two spires, neither particularly high nor dreaming, stood on either side of the short end-wall, where the entrance door, a bright blue arched double sliding door stood out like lipstick on the face of an otherwise unmade-up, wrinkly old drag-queen. On the steps and on the landing outside the entrance a throng of people were milling about. The 9am service had just finished and the 11am was about to begin. Some were coming others going, many just standing around talking, shouting, laughing. M stopped in his tracks and didn't quite know what to make of it. The backdrop was old Victorian faux gothic, the foreground Africa, the mix Commonwealth, the mismatch strangely British. As M moved closer he heard them talking loudly in their braying African languages, or English with strong West-African accents. They laughed at things M did not find funny. Many were dressed in large, flowing, brightly coloured habits, or shiny suits with bright shirts and very pointy shoes. Interspersing the sea of West-Africana was East Africans, Asians, South Americans and even some pink-pale whities looking anaemic and sullenly disoriented, like a vicar at a workingmen's club.

As M entered the tiny lobby, jammed packed with people, books, video tapes, audio tapes, boxes, magazines and a reception desk, he noticed the lady behind the latter. She would have been a beautiful lady when she was young. A *very* long time ago. Proudly she clung to the memory of good looks by sporting a giant wig of shiny black curls almost enveloping her entirely, as she was not very large. M fancied she looked like a hair-troll, only noticing two giant trainers sticking out at the bottom of the wig, and a heavily made up wrinkly face emerging from the middle of the plastic hair mass. M blessed himself that there were people in existence this near to him so totally untouched by the depressing severity of grey Scandinavian naturality. The lips circling the protruding teeth were deep red and high gloss and M could not help falling deeply in love with such a lovely specimen of anti-Norwegianness. He managed to tear his stare away in time to see Zelma darting up the winding staircase, having decided that there was a better chance of a seat in the gallery.

He sat down on a fold-down plush, velveteen covered chair – that he later learned had been procured from the Royal Opera House when the latter had had new chairs fitted – and noticed sadly that the gothic exterior had nothing to do with the tatty, practical but run-down, dirty, unprettiness of the interior. Torn, grubby carpets, miscoloured walls scattered with marks, and on the floor of the main hall a mass of brown plastic chairs. It all looked tired and shabby. The stage area suddenly filled with people, including the band, and a man said a few words of welcome before everyone was invited to stand up and praise the Lord, which they all did. The little stage was full of people, drums, guitars, keyboards, a lectern, chairs and various sound equipment. Two massive speakers suspended from a rafter blasted out loud electric worship music and the congregation joined in with such a roar of enthusiasm that M thought the roof or the old building would crumble over their heads. The pastors came on. Three white and one black. The singing went on and on, with big, fat, black ladies dancing and swinging their enormous rumps to the rhythm of the music. M could have sworn the entire building was swaying and he couldn't help enjoying himself.

Make a joyful noise unto God
Psalm 66; 1

The speaker was the Senior Pastor Walter C. Leakey. Pastor Leakey had taken over the leadership of the Chelsea Chapel from Will Davies, a highly popular, little Welsh minister, who grew the attendance from a few hundred a week to several thousands each Sunday. His recipe was simple: make the house of the Lord as inclusive as possible without compromising on the theology. He encouraged the start-up of special sub-groups for various special interests; national groups; creative groups (which had developed into a department of Creative Ministries in the Bible Institute) professional groups; a group for those afflicted by gayness: for their rectification (so to speak) but in a spirit of relative tolerance. There was an Ethiopian group, a Ghanaian, Kenyan, Sierra Leonean, Spanish, Italian, Chinese, Japanese; and even one for people who worked in the city. Some of these groups had grown so much that they required their own meeting space in their local area; and so from this had sprung the system of satellite churches, with Chelsea Chapel as the parent company and the smaller community churches as the subsidiaries.

This flurry of activity had seen attendance over the network surpass 10,000 each Sunday. The then assistants pastor Walter Leakey had launched the campaign '2,000 By the Year 2000'; its goal to have a total of 2,000 satellite churches by the turn of the millennium. Also, as a brainchild of Leakey, they had certain key centres linked up by an actual satellite TV-link one Sunday a month, to strengthen the bond to the mothership. The satellite broadcast was additionally taken by affiliated churches in Scandinavia, Germany and France, making the service a truly international affair. All services were videotaped and express-copied to make it available, along with the church's books and audio tapes, for sale straight after each service, overseen by a former BBC employee: Ben Carton. So, despite the shabbiness and general chaotic run-down appearance of the place they ran a pretty well oiled religious business. In a strange way M felt this added to their appeal. The traditional churches had become little more than museums coated in a sugary icing of politically correct lefty platitudes. He was looking forward to studying at this successful church's Bible Institute and learn how to run a modern, living church that cared more for the eternal soul of the parishioners, than the eco-health of a transient planet or the distribution of material goods.

For ye have the poor always with you
MATTHEW XXVI; 11

Chapter III

In which our hero finds a job he really wants and visits friends

As the electric worship-band rounded off the service a mass exodus flowed through the narrow doors and stairwells and people seemed to issue forth through every opening in the building until the front landing and the pavement around the church were quite swamped. Zelma had excused herself to go and speak Spanish with fellow South Americans. M joined the stream leading to the front landing, where a railing ran along, and positioned himself on the far corner of the railing, observing people as they came out. A large, African lady in a resplendent dress was telling off two small, identical looking boys in white suits. Dark brown faces with huge, white teeth.

"What would my mother have made of this?" wondered M.

A scruffy looking elderly white man shuffled by clutching a Tesco plastic bag, probably containing his Bible and some notepaper. He must be English, thought M. Then again... A beautiful, tall, blond lady floated by. Two African fellows came out laughing. One kept repeating, "yezzir, yezzir, yezzir" and the other seemed to think this hilariously funny.

The next service wasn't starting for another two hours, so after a while the place emptied. A strange feeling crept over M. Back in his little home church the after service time was the best part. It was the time everybody secretly looked forward to. Nobody would admit as much, of course. That would be an admission of how absurd, irrelevant and tedious the repeat of the same old songs, the never-ending sermons and the barren prayers actually were. But you could see it in people's faces. The way their faces would light up the moment the pastor gave the benediction, and someone would invite the rest to come over to their house for coffee and cakes, or someone would steal off to the local Chinese. Most often, M and his pals would cram into Georg's green Ford, and take off to his flat to drink lapsang souchong – prepared carefully and in perfect adherence to the ancient rules of proper tea-making – and listen to jazz.

If the weather was good perhaps drive out to the nearby coast and wander about aimlessly and happily with the fresh sea breeze ruffling one's hair. Georg was a drummer in M's band. He owned an old Gretch drum kit that today would be called 'vintage'. Sundays were long days filled with the unproblematic togetherness of male friendship. They were brethren, saved by the grace of God, *in* this world but not *of* it. They were strangers in the land, sojourners through hostile landscapes, facing the enemy together. Standing on that landing in Chelsea, London, England, all by himself, M felt terribly alone. There was no one to go with and nowhere to go. He was simply all by himself, and it was getting cloudy and colder. He went back inside. The walking wig had just put up a notice on the board. M went over and had a look. 'Receptionist wanted for church's new head offices. Training given. Part time.' M asked for a piece of scrap paper and a pen and jotted down the details. He knew the Bible College would be in the same building as the new offices, a large building the church had just started leasing on the edge of London's western suburbia. It would therefore be extremely convenient to work and study in the same building. M felt a surge of optimism, and set off for home, forgetting Zelma and the other services yet to come. He spent that Sunday afternoon writing and rewriting the application, getting the paperwork photocopied at the local newsagent at 10 pence a sheet, and, having greatly inflated the voluntary work he had done for the old home church, he was finally ready to have the cover letter typed up. M wondered how he was going to do that on a Sunday, when he remembered his old pastor Sigmund and his wife Gerd. He had only seen them briefly when he arrived; they had arranged the accommodation with Zelma for him. Since then M had been busy, but they had said he could come at anytime if he needed anything, and now he did. He called and learned they would be at home the rest of the day; he could come when he liked.

M gathered up the papers in a folder and jumped on a bus that took him to a Piccadilly line station, where he set off for Uxbridge station, the last stop on one branch of the blue line. Sigmund, and his wife Gerd, had been in Christian ministry for almost a quarter of a century. In this time Sigmund had built up Happy Life church, presided over its split into two factions, and in the end realised that as 'no prophet is accepted in his own hometown'. His ambition for a worldwide, international apostolic ministry was not going to come to fruition in the little parochial town of fisheries and fjords on the west coast of Norway. He'd had a couple of speaking engagements in other countries and from this he concluded he was called to make an international base somewhere where his talents would be appreciated. This led to negotiations being opened with the Chelsea Chapel and the Metropolitan Satellite network. In the end a transfer was agreed and he was engaged as a full-time paid pastor of Uxbridge Christian Fellowship, consisting of less than a dozen people, mainly pensioners. Sigmund had made it clear he was not primarily a pastor, but more importantly: *an apostle*. This removed some of the pressure to be 'pastoral' whilst still making it imperative to speak at great lengths to anyone forced to listen.

His style of speaking could perhaps explain the dwindling number of willing listeners. He would normally start by quoting numerous passages from the Bible, often with no apparent connection, and often from study Bibles with clunky word-for-word translations from the Greek (he had no Greek himself). His understanding of his own shortcomings as a public speaker was non-existent. He had no formal education beyond the seven years of elementary schooling that was the norm in Norway when he was young, and had obtained a theological understanding of sorts by reading a vast number of selective books, mostly written by the sort of preachers who themselves had no formal theological education. Was he ever embarrassed by the lack of formal education? On the contrary. It was the job of the Holy Spirit to instruct, and the less his own intellect got in the way of his sprit to hear from the Holy Spirit, the better. That is not to say that Sigmund was simplistic. Far from it. Indeed, very, very far from it. He loved discussing all sorts of issues at great length and depth, and the less his interlocutor knew of the subject under discussion, the more convincing Sigmund was. He was well able to break out from the conformity of the mainstream mind-set and come up with original and interesting contributions. The perfect absence of logical stringency, combined with gaping holes in his knowledge meant most contributions could be questioned, but as he surrounded himself with even less knowledgeable followers they weren't.

Notwithstanding, he had always been very kind to M, more like an uncle than a pastor, since M joined Happy Life Church, and M thought his wife Gerd was as close as any mortal human being can come to angelic perfection. Always considerate, mild and wise, with an apparently inexhaustible patience she kept Sigmund organised, ensured he got to where he was supposed to get to, at the right time and in the right clothes. Quietly she made sure their impractical life became possible, and surrounded Sigmund's childlike explorer-urge with a calm, protective predictability. *She* was his rock.

And I say also unto thee, that thou art Peter, and upon this rock I
will build my church; and the gates of hell
shall not prevail against it.
MATTHEW XVI; 18

Pastor Sigmund hooted the horn as he turned the car around to let M in.

"Good day, or should I perhaps say 'good evening' rather? Get in, get in, it's the church that paid for the car, it's been a nightmare to learn to drive on the left, and of course I had to get my license changed to a British one, you know it is actually an EU-license now, he-he". "*Most people* (this was quite a favourite expression of his, pronounced with much disdain in his voice) think the EU is something sinister and dangerous, remember how all Christians voted against it in Norway, contributing to the 'no' in the referendum, because they believe it is the rise of the new Roman empire as prophesied in the Book of Revelation, from which the Beast shall forge his powers – and it may very well be of course – but all the while it is there it's convenient for spreading the gospel, making it easier for Christians to travel. Remember the apostle Paul: when he was arrested he was a Roman citizen and that helped him a lot, so I think there is a message for us in that".

As Sigmund concentrated on getting through a roundabout the 'wrong way' and on the 'wrong side' of the road, M wanted to mention that he had actually voted 'yes' to the European Fellowship in '94, and that he had, contrary to everyone else he knew in the non-conformist Christian community in town, worn a 'vote YES' button and argued strongly that although he was in principle against super-states, joining in the free trade across borders would be good for Norway. He then thought he would follow up with asking after Gerd. Unfortunately he was too slow off the mark.

"You know what they call these things here? *Roundabout*! Ha-ha! That is just so funny, *roundabout* the Christmas tree. *Most people* learning English don't realise that is what they're called. And *this* (he switched on the indicator) is not called the 'blinking light', as *most people* would think, but *indicators*."

"And how's Gerd?" M managed to shoot in as Sigmund drew breath.

"Oh she's… er… OK, I think. You know I am having such great difficulties with the church I am leading now," Sigmund said as he went through a red light.

"Oh, I thought it was ideal for you: you get paid full-time, free car, easy to travel to other places in the world from Heathrow…"

Sigmund cut him off: "Yes, yes, yes, but they demand too much of me as a *pastor*. They need *pastoral care*."

The last two words came out of his mouth with venomous emphasis. I really don't have the motivation for it. There is no inspiration for me in listening to other people whining. And you know, the church in Norway was a youth church, full of vibrant, young people. These guys are old, stale and set in their ways. A few years ago they had a conflict or other, and the hard feelings still prevail. Lots of bad blood and all that. Well, obviously I have had experience with church breakups, which is partly why the Metropolitan Church headquarters wanted me to take on this one, but you've got to move on. Can't get stuck in the past. No good. *Most people* don't realise this."

With this he veered the car across the road just missing an oncoming lorry.

*And God hath set some in the church, first apostles, secondarily
prophets, thirdly teachers, after that miracles, then gifts of
healings, helps, governments, diversities of tongues.*
1 Corinthians XIII; 28

He had talked his way from Uxbridge to the sprawling neighbourhood in which he lived with Gerd, where row upon depressing row of newish identikit red-brick terraced houses were thrown together, its proximity to surrounding trading estates being a greater asset than any natural beauty of this sub-suburban wasteland. Cars lined both sides of the cul-de-sac's winding street, and M wondered if any neighbour ever asked another for a cup of sugar here. Some of the houses were divided into two flats: ground and first floor. Sigmund and Gerd had been provided with one such first floor flat by the church, right at the end of the cul-de-sac. Gerd came out and greeted M in her quietly friendly way, accompanied by the continuing narrative of Sigmund.

"The church got us this house, or flat really. It's OK. Very small, but there's English houses for you. Gerd! Some coffee perhaps? Really strong! You like it strong? I need it strong. I am turning the days around. I work better during the night. The inspiration flows better. There's the machine."

They had climbed a very narrow staircase, entered a tiny hall and arrived in a small living room with a sunken looking grey sofa, a round dining table all surrounded by off-white walls with no pictures. Sigmund pointed to a museum piece standing on a rickety little side table, almost drowned by stacks upon stacks of notepaper, books and writing pads, and instructed M in its use. As Gerd brought refreshments, M managed to type out his CV and cover letter, being offered a continuous stream of helpful advice from Sigmund.

"You see, what you need to do when you're marketing yourself, selling yourself, is to focus on the other person. Say 'you' a lot. Don't focus on *your* own needs. They couldn't care less what *you* need. This is what *most people* don't understand."

At one point M had to ask Sigmund to relent. "Sigmund, I just need to think a little bit, could you…"

"Oh sorry, yes. Nothing worse than people yapping away when you're trying to think, it is the worst thing I know".

"Perhaps you should be quiet then," said his wife gently, but firmly, not looking up from the book she was reading.

Immediately Sigmund started whispering: "I know. Terrible. I talk too much. Anyway, I shall be quiet." He picked up a book, made some witty comment to himself that nobody heard, giggled a little, and then started reading, and muttering as he read.

"It's a book of positive statements, if you're wondering why I am muttering. I'm sure you'd like it. *The Lord is within me, His spirit dwells on the inside of me and I can do all things through Christ who strengthens me.* Good stuff eh?"

Gerd looked up from her book.

"Oh, I'll be quiet now." Sigmund said with a boyish smile of apology.

M proofread a little longer than necessary to extend the quiet, but in the end he had to press 'print', and as the old printer beat the words out with loud rasping and clonkety clicking, the floodgates of oral flatulence reopened and all the myriad musings Sigmund had had to dam up for twenty minutes came streaming out. M thankfully felt the need to do a necessary errand and asked for directions.

"Into the hall, first on the right," Gerd said, as Sigmund carried on regardless. As M stepped into the bathroom, he couldn't believe his eyes. The floor of the toilet was covered with a thick, beige carpet. The sort of carpet one might in Norway have had in the bedroom in the 1970s. But on a bathroom floor? M quickly, and carefully, did what he had to do and got out of there.

"Sigmund, there's carpet on the bathroom floor!" M said as he re-entered the living room.

"Ha-ha! I know. Gave us a bit of start too. The English are crazy you know. They love their carpets everywhere. I wonder why they didn't put it on the walls as well!"

Gerd had prepared some supper, and they ate and listened to Sigmund.

As he drove M back to the station, Sigmund said: "I know what to do with this church".

"Really?" M replied.

"Yes. I will continue to take the salary they pay me, try to keep them happy in their whining, maintaining their little gatherings like they're used to, and start a new ministry and church separate from this one".

"But how will they feel about your building a church on the salary they pay?"

"Oh they won't know. Not that I am hiding it of course, but I'm just not actively marketing it internally. Why should I?"

"Well…"

"I know, *they* pay my salary, but if I am to be efficient in the Kingdom of God I must do what gives *me* inspiration, what fires up *my* spirit. This is what *most people* don't understand".

"Yes, I suppose you must," M said, and then thanked for the loan of the machine, and felt a sense of relief when he sat down on the train. He sighed as he reflected on why he didn't believe Sigmund would succeed with his new church, or the old church, or any church for that matter.

Except the Lord build the house, they labour in vain
that build it
Psalm 127; 1

CHAPTER IV

In which our hero starts working and we are introduced to his boss

A few days after sending in his application M was called for an interview. When he entered the room he felt confident the job would be his. There was a sense of gratefulness in their behaviour towards him, or at least that is how their brand of politeness made M feel. Afterwards M could not remember what they'd asked him, except why he wanted to work for a big church like the Chelsea Chapel? M smiled a lot and said, partly because it was true and partly because he thought it was what they wanted to hear, that he thought he had a pastoral calling.

"And you think working in a big church will help you learn about the practical aspects of the ministry?" Charlie Hatkinson had helpfully finished M's sentence. Mr Hatkinson had jet black hair, with two streaks of grey running from the left temple back, combed in an '80s Wall Street fashion straight back, with lots of something in it to make it shiny. He was youngish, late 20s or early 30s perhaps, and the senior pastor's protégé.

Also present, in a way that seemed to take up no space, was a Pinocchio-thin man with a large head. His hair was cut very short, he had the shadow of a moustache and large, metal-rim glasses, of the sort that unfashionable people think are fashionable but know are sensible. He was Mr Robert Teethall, the church's administrator. He sat, legs crossed, fidgeting nervously with papers on his lap, looking to confident Charlie to lead the questioning. Next to Mr Teethall sat an Asian lady. Neither young nor old, never smiling nor frowning, she seemed to defer to her male colleagues. M would get to know Tracey Chung very well indeed, she was the reception manageress.

M went back to the jobcentre where he had registered. He informed a skinny, bearded man that he was now in employment and no longer required to be on the books, nor receive the jobseekers allowance. The skinny man seemed almost disappointed.

"Oh well, that is good news, isn't it?" he said disingenuously.

"Yes, very. Thank you for your help".

"Not at all," the man said as he moved some papers, then looked up at M. "*Do* come back if you need to".

"Thank you," was all M managed to say, and it was enough. There was an oppressive atmosphere, as if the demon of the Welfare state tried to suck the life-juice out of him. He hurried out and closed the door behind him. He took from his inner pocket his return ticket to Norway and tore it up. He knew, whatever happened, he would never go back.

Therefore take no thought, saying, What shall we eat? or, What
shall we drink? or, Wherewithal shall we be clothed?
(For after all these things do the Gentiles seek:) for your heavenly
Father knoweth that ye have need of all these things.
But seek ye first the kingdom of God, and his righteousness; and all
these things shall be added unto you.
Take therefore no thought for the morrow: for the morrow shall

take thought for the things of itself.
Sufficient unto the day is the evil thereof.
MATTHEW VII; 31 – 34

The offices of Chelsea Chapel were larger than expected. Apart from the suite of offices containing the senior minister and his entourage: his PA, his secretary, his two assistants, and the second pastor; there was a separate pastoral division, a youth division, a music division, a missions division, a cell-group division, a finance division, a satellite-church division, and of course an operations divisions, within which M's new job sorted.

The operations division had only recently come into being, from what had up until then simply been *Administration*, when the church had created the position of General Manager of Operations especially for Mr Pete Crowley, a big, fat man – fat in the same way as the hard man at the milk depot – with a bulldog's face. M sensed immediately, and quite rightly, that there was great respect for Mr Crowley, even a hint of fear. He soon discovered why; apart from his constant frown and formidable physical presence, he had the power to sign purchase orders, as well as to hire and fire people. Obviously the latter didn't apply to the more senior staff, but even so; if they wanted anyone hired or fired in their departments they would have to go through Pete Crowley, General Manager of Operations. Crowley had grown up in the church, as the son of a lay minister. Religion was part of his DNA, but he was not a religious type. He was a tough, rugby-playing fighter. He had the appearance of a bully, but he never bullied, nor stood idly by looking at those too weak to defend themselves being bullied. He'd got himself into many scrapes with his teachers over fistfights that he invariably won. His father always supported him, knowing that his son would never be the first to hit. Pete Crawley resented the attempt to contain his fighting sprit in a meek, feminised religion, and once he moved out to make his own way in the world, his faith was buried, as the mustard seed grain, deep in very fertile ground, waiting for the right propagator to set it growing. Being hard working and sociable he soon found himself a successful sales-rep for a large corporation, and soon after that regional manager. Then he moved from one successful managerial position to the next until he had reached executive seniority that left little room for further professional growth. As long as he had been infernally busy he had had a kind of purpose: moving up and on, and he hadn't had to think about why....

He now found himself in a situation where he was one of the youngest members of an exclusive, executive golf club, but without any further goals to reach. To the surface small bubbles started suddenly to rise and pop; all is vanity, except the Lord build the house, the love of money is the root of all evil, etc. His wife, herself more a cabbage than a flower in the garden of God, with no time for golf clubs and such like, had kept herself faithful to the church. When one day a revivalist preacher visited from America, she told her husband he'd better come along. He, partly out of matrimonial duty, partly out of an inbred feeling of guilt, and partly in search of something to fill the growing void in his soul, went along. The words of the preacher fell like blows upon open wounds;

"You carry on in your sinful ways with no reference to the love of God in your life, you carry on making plans ignoring the great plan God has for you, God gave his only begotten son for you, what have you given him? At best a few pounds for the church roof!"

This last point stung Pete, because he had written out a cheque – with an amount that for most church members would've seemed a lot, but for him was a modest amount – for just such a purpose not long ago.

The seed had met its propagator, and when the call was made at the end of the sermon to come forward, amidst a tremulous organ playing *The Old*

Rugged Cross, Pete was moved, rose and came forward to bend his knees alongside other repentant prodigals. The experience Pete had at this point was unlike any other. Although he had grown up in church, and always believed in God in his own way, he had never experienced being 'born again'. Now he did. A strange sensation of joy and satisfaction seemed to descend upon him like a bright, warm mist, spreading from his heart to the uttermost extremities of his body. It was as if a light stood before him and he heard a voice saying, "follow me".

All he could say was, "yes Lord, yes Lord". He kept repeating, "yes Lord," as tears streamed down his cheeks. Many of the regular churchgoers were themselves moved to tears by the sight of this tough, hard, seemingly self-sufficient man, humbled by the Love of God.

And he spake many things unto them in parables, saying, Behold, a
sower went forth to sow;
and when he sowed, some seeds fell by the wayside, [...]
but other fell into good ground, and brought forth fruit, some a
hundredfold, some sixtyfold, some thirtyfold.
Who hath ears to hear, let him hear."
MATTHEW XIII; 3 – 9

In the wake of this experience Pete felt a new man. He was dissatisfied with working 'in the world', and started looking for ways in which he could use his considerable experience and knowledge for the good of God's Kingdom. After a while the opportunity arose as the American itinerant speaker and fundraiser par excellence Jacob Cherubo was opening up a European office, to coordinate his activities on that continent, as well as in the Middle and Far East. The self-styled *doctor* Cherubo travelled the world, preaching wherever a huge crowd of believers could be gathered and collection boxes be passed around.

He had surmised, correctly, that Europe was full of believers with strong currencies. Cherubo was originally of Jewish descent but had become a born-again Christian in his youth. He had started his preaching career travelling from town to town, city to city, often sleeping in the back of his beaten up Oldsmobile. And in a religious echo of the American dream he build his ministry slowly but surely until it reached the global mega-proportion it now had. From his base in San Diego, where several hundred staff busily worked, he ran a radio and television channel, a magazine, as well as production and sales of books, audio and videotapes. He had his own private aeroplane, and he never travelled anywhere without his wife and his own private organist. The organist would play the organ dynamically during Cherubo's speeches. When Cherubo whispered, the organ lay low in the bass frequencies, vibrating its way into people's hearts. When Cherubo raised his voice – sometimes to a screaming pitch – the Hammond B-3 organ went into a high, tremulous descant, screaming with its master like a caged spirit. The worship leader was a black gospel singer of the old generation, called Arty. He had a gruff bass voice that grabbed you by the scruff of your neck and pulled you up on your feet. Then it punched you in the solar plexus depositing an irresistible urge to dance and move about, clap your hands and shout for joy. Anyone who ever had the privilege of witnessing the Jacob Cherubo road show could readily understand why he did not want to depend on local sources for his back up. Cherubo's strategy of ministry was to preach the gospel in far flung countries, financed by his 'wealthier' supporters, many of whom lived in the poorest inner city areas of America; clinging to the promise of a hundred-fold return on their tithes and offerings to God and Cherubo. The doctor's renown had even reached the little church in the little town on the coast of Norway where M had belonged. A friend of M, an intelligent man suffering from schizophrenia, was a great fan of Cherubo and bought his books and audiotapes and sent money. One day, after having responded to an appeal to send money, he asked M for some help. Everyone who had donated above a certain amount received in return a little cloth and a tiny receptacle of oil, both having been blessed by the great man of God and thus acquired the status of prayer-cloth and anointing oil. M was asked to help administer the pre-paid blessing, and to touch his friend's forehead whilst praying. M readily played his part and poured the few drops of oil to the little piece of cloth and touched his friend's forehead, whereupon the latter fell unto the floor and started speaking in other tongues. M was unsure whether it was the spirit in the cloth or the schizophrenia in the friend that had caused the reaction, but just in case it was a *buy one get one free* blessing he did touch his own forehead, with no tangible reaction.

What Cherubo had discovered though, was the psychology of self-interest: if donors received a little token of their giving they would be more willing to give, and secondly he had discovered that Europe was full of relatively wealthy Christians willing to pour money into his operations. It was around this time that Pete Crowley was hired as Director of European Operations for the Jacob Cherubo Ministries. His task was to organise a 'Mission To Europe', starting with a weeklong convention in Earls Court Arena, London. The stated rationale for this 'mission' was that Europe, once the part of the world that sent missionaries to the rest of the world, spreading the gospel, was now in danger of de-Christianisation. It had to be re-Christianised.

Together with his friend, Georg, and a delegation of about a dozen from his home church, M travelled to London to congregate with 15,000 other saints in the six day long spiritual bonanza every August throughout the early '90s. Little did M know that the man organising the whole thing would be his boss by the latter part of the decade. Pete Crowley's role within the Jacob Cherubo ministries developed from covering Europe only, to cover the worldwide itinerary outside the USA. He criss-crossed the globe first class with a company credit card, worked a lot and ate a lot. Cherubo was a demanding man to work for. Pete had to be available at all hours to travel to any part of the world, to be the ready recipient of barrages of abuse and public humiliation. After every meeting Pete had to personally supervise the counting of the collection, and after the counting had been done Doctor Cherubo would come and take the cash, countersign the accounts, and assume full control over every penny. He half-jokingly said of himself:

"Doctor Cherubo (he always spoke of himself in the third person) may be a Christian, but he is still a Jew".

The strain of the constant pressure eventually got to Pete. At the Mission To Europe in 1996 he discovered from Walter Leakey – the new Senior Pastor of Chelsea Chapel – that they were looking for a Head of Operations. After taking on a large new building, expanding the staff, and developing a media department, they wanted someone to pull all the diverse strings together. Pastor Leakey, having recently taken over from the jovial Will Davies, wanted to streamline his organisation and make it more professional. An understanding formed between the two men, and nine months later Pete Crowley was duly announced as the General Manager of Operations of the Chelsea Chapel and the London Metropolitan Church Network. A very far cry from the humble deacon, shuffling about saving the butt ends of candles, Mr Crowley was given a suite of offices, which incorporated Mr Teethall, the senior church administrator, Mr Oliver Davidsen, operations assistant, and Miss Tina Thompson, PA to the general manager of operations. Also reporting directly to the general manager of operations was the head of Dovetail Media, the department of the church dealing with the church magazine, book publishing and marketing, video and audio production, and other essential church functions. This department was at its core charged with the task of selling the message. If Walter Leakey uttered it, Dovetail hawked it.

M's responsibilities included answering the telephone and redirecting the calls, receiving visitors, sorting the post and putting it into the right pigeon holes, franking outgoing mail and making it ready for the postman – an Essex boy who was very concerned that the weight should not be a single gramme over the 11 kilos determined by 'an ee-yeu die-ractive' – and any other task that might be deemed necessary. The church offices were not a highly formal environment. But M made it his business to appear perfectly groomed and turned-out every day in a tie and jacket, answering the phone in a friendly tone, but also with robotic precision according to his instructions: "Good morning [or afternoon, as the case may be], Chelsea Chapel offices this is M speaking, how may I help you?"

M wrote to his friends in the old home church in Norway and told them proudly of his success in securing employment in the metropolitan super church. He was working in the hub, at the very heart of the biggest and most influential independent church in Europe. When people phoned this eponymous church it was M's voice they met heard, it was his greeting that gave them their first impression. His friends were impressed, but not surprised. In their eyes, M always seemed to naturally assume leadership in a group and become the default point of gravity in a party. M was aware of this ability, and he liked it. You gain much by being good looking, but acting as if you're not. M had never thought himself particularly good looking, and so he compensated by smiling a lot. But he struggled with the Christian commandment to love one's neighbour. He did, however, have something else which might be as good as love (or even better) and that was *loyalty*.

Although M's father had a successful business and was well off financially, his background culturally was working class. From apprentice at a shipyard, he had worked his way up to Chief Engineer on a large international cargo ship, and then started his own engineering company; his values and sensitivities were working class of the 1st Order. His greatest respect was reserved for those who were good at something; "he's a craftsman," was the highest praise M's father could bestow upon any living being. The working class of the 1st Order's code is one of honesty, directness, strength (physical and mental), chivalry, and loyalty. Honesty in that you say what you mean and stand by it, whoever you speak to. You do not change your opinion on a subject to suit the company, or soften the message to please your superiors, or to be kind to your subordinates. That would be 'false kindness', and falseness was a despicable vice. Directness in that you would state clearly what you meant, without beating about the bush, not being afraid to confront disagreement. The exception would be women and sometimes children. Directness was both about saying something straight out, without the use of euphemisms, and also being able to take it on the chin when someone spoke back directly.

If someone was fat, you would call him *fat*. If someone was slow, you would call him *stupid*. The corresponding vice was oversensitivity. The virtue of directness leads to a robust, sometimes even cruel, sense of humour preying on the weaknesses of the object of the joke. Far from ignoring a sore point, salt would be generously administered. But, as we know, although salt can stem the rot it can also create hardness and stale bitterness. Strength was very important. Physical strength was admired (M's elder brother took to pumping iron in the gym to get his muscles growing: a modern fad his father despised), mental strength was respected, and taken as a given with being a *man*. (A real *man*, as opposed to just a man, was one who embodied all of these values). In strength you, as a *man*, should be able to provide for your family all their physical needs, as well as protect them and yourself against any physical aggression. You should be able to carry all the worries, without burdening the womenfolk. This leads us to Chivalry. Equality of the sexes was for the working class of the first order an evil subversion of the family society, a subjugation of mandom and a corrosion of womanhood. M's mother would decry the horrible red-stockings of the women's lib asking rhetorically "would they be men?" But much as M's father disliked the *movement,* and the changes to society, "forcing both parents to work is wrong to the children". He did admire strong women individually, who were good at what they were doing. They fell into the 'craftsmen' category. From Norway he followed the career of Margaret Thatcher approvingly, silently bestowing upon her the status of honorary *man.* You had to assert yourself in this environment, you had to learn to argue for your views and ridicule your opponent, to be strong and tough and resilient. But no matter how hard you fought your corner, how much you disagreed, at the end of the day your loyalty was with the family and your close friends. For M, being of an academic disposition, it was necessary to rise above some of the more primitive, unreflective sentiments of this Class. His was a higher order: one of words, their nuances and effects; a world of poetry, of art, of literature, of music, of philosophy, of religious mysteries.

He pined for his old family's illustrious past: their prime ministers, bishops, writers, composers and civil servants. He regarded the present dip into working middle class an anomaly to be restored. His was an aristocratic spirit, embarrassed at his family's lack of appreciation of classical music and the finer arts, yet finding there was an honesty in the love of simple music and simple pleasures. The two strands of his background culminated in an overbearing distaste for members of the struggling middling classes, with their petty little sensitivities and false politenes and middle ground politics. Norway was a middle-country. Moderately capitalistic, moderately socialistic, moderately religious. with moderate secularism. There were no extremes in Norway:

nothing extremely good and nothing extremely bad, just extremely middle ground. But the middle ground was never M's comfortable home ground.

I know thy works, that thou art neither cold nor hot: I would
thou wert cold or hot.
So then because thou art lukewarm, and neither cold nor hot, I will
spew thee out of my mouth.
Because thou sayest, I am rich, and increased with goods, and have
need of nothing; and knowest not that thou art wretched, and
miserable, and poor, and blind, and naked
REVELATION, IV; 15 – 17

The working class virtue of loyalty was the one that stuck deep in M, and one person more than any other had M's total loyalty, and in turn reciprocated it: his best friend Georg. In Norway at the time this was the name of an old man. Your uncle would be called Georg, or more possibly your grandfather. Yet, although Georg was only six years older than M, the name fit him perfectly. He was a sort of old man in a young man's body, in an old man's shirt. The impression of old manliness was strengthened by Georg having very thin blonde hair. It was white to the point of translucency. When he had just had his haircut he seemed completely bald until you got close-up. Just before the haircut, it looked as if he was wearing a fluffy cloud. He had calm pale blue eyes; a rather long thin nose and a tiny mouth, sitting in a face of slightly puffed cheeks. His neck was thin, his shoulders narrow, and his body free of athletic traces. He dressed in brown corduroys, checked or floral shirts, and a tweed jacket with leather pads on the elbows. It was he who introduced M to the proper art of tea making. Georg always stocked a selection of Chinese teas, such as Jasmine, Blue Flower, and the smoky Lapsang Souchong, M's favourite. He would invariably prepare the loose leaf tea with pedantic precision, slowly and systematically like a priest conducting a sacred rite. Georg had also brought jazz into M's life; whilst M could boast of having brought classical into Georg's. Each retained their points of gravity with the music they brought into the mix, accepting and being open to the other's contributions.

Together they had discovered early black gospel music, which, with its earthy, bluesy jazzness, became the chief inspiration for them both in the band they had together with two others. Georg was witty where M was sarcastic. He was subtly humorous where M performed outrageous impressions, he was pragmatic where M was highly principled, he appreciated art where M wanted to be a great artist, he dressed youthfully conservative where M wore a black beret, round glasses and smoked a pipe. Georg was quiet, a little shy, and always perfectly polite, where M was noisily extrovert, self-confidently taking centre stage and sometimes more than a little rude. They understood and appreciated each other. And as they had no need or want to outshine each other, they were the other's greatest fan. The slightest nod and wink was enough for the other person to know exactly what was thought and meant. Their humour was so finely tuned that when looking at the same object they both laughed at the same time at precisely the same thing.

It was not without reason that M had given his entire collection of European and Russian art-house films to Georg, when he moved to London. Had it been hard for M to leave his friend behind? Not really, after all it was *London* that was waiting for him. And Georg acknowledged the allure of this city; indeed he cared very much for it himself. So perhaps there was a certain pain. But it was deep down, unspoken of. Unmentioned in every way but perhaps the odd bits of silence and a look away. But M had no time for subtlety; he was busy staging the script for the next episode of his life.

M. W. HAGERUP

CHAPTER V

In which we are introduced to the pastor and our hero
gets himself into a bit of a scrape

The phone rang incessantly that day. M had developed a studied automation in his friendly replies:

"GoodmorningChelseaChapelheadofficeMspeakinghowmayIhelpyou?"

There were times so many called all he could say was, "I'll be with you in a moment," put it on hold, do the same with the next, and the next, and the next, go back to the first, direct the call, new call on hold, next, direct, next, on hold, direct, on hold, etcetera, etcetera. As the phones calmed down towards the later afternoon M answered in his normal automatrix manner.

"I will tell you exactly how you can help me," said a familiar voice. It was Georg's.

"Hey my dear friend! How are you doing?" M answered, feeling very pleased with hearing his friend's voice again, and stealing a break from the daily routines.

"Thank you fine. Listen, I'm coming to London next month."

"Great! Coming for the conference?"

"Of course. Now, you wrote you had moved into a studio-flat…" M knew what was coming and welcomed it.

"Yes indeed. Finally out of the clutches of Zelma. You want to come and stay?"

"That would be very nice, thank you," said Georg politely. "But I need to warn you I am planning to stay an extra week, to have some time to do things, you know."

"Of course, my friend, goes without saying. Looking forward to it. It's in Ealing Broadway, so it's a little bit of a track to get into London, but at least it's on the Central Line. But Georg, you know my Bible College studies will commence straight after the conference, so you may want to come the week before. That way I can work mornings and have the afternoons with you."

"OK, I will bear it in mind when I order the tickets."

"Did you know I met Sigmund?"

"Oh really? How was he?"

"Talkative, as ever. But the great thing is he's got a car, Georg. Perhaps we could persuade him to take us for a ride somewhere out of London. I've heard Christchurch is supposed to be very nice."

"Sounds superb. OK, well I'll talk to you again with the details before I travel. This is getting expensive, so bye for now."

And with that the old voice was gone. M felt a momentary pang of loss.

M could sometimes be awfully careless. His sometimes cruel humour was at times expressed with his talent for drawing caricatures, an ability that had stood him in good stead in school, where his cartoons lampooning teachers and fellow pupils had earned him a certain status. Some fellows begged him to draw them, whilst the merciless depiction of teachers as vultures, weaklings or grumps secured a popular following. One fellow pupils, substantially bigger than M had once threatened direct action after becoming the involuntary star of a comic strip, but M managed to talk his way out of it. Now, as receptionist he had an orchestral view to his new masters in their comings and goings.

The Senior Pastor, the Reverend Walter C. Leakey, was a man of medium height and with a very slender frame. He wore his mouse-brown hair combed back in a large wave, with a thread of silver (thought to be natural) going through it from the left temple curling upwards.

In his youth he had trained as a ballet dancer, and this was still very much part of his identity. He moved in a curiously feminine way, holding his nose skywards, seemingly taking directions by sniffing the air above him. He would walk stretching one foot in front of the other, almost in the manner of a *tendu devant*, and thus bounce along swiftly, arms swinging, until he met someone he wanted to speak to, theatrically smiling whilst lowering his face, raising the face again and looking away. Then, to express favour he would look intensely into his interlocutor's eyes and renew the prefabricated grin, or to express disfavour would glance around looking irritated and bored.

In his sermons Leakey would wave his arms in large, dramatic movements, raising and lowering his voice in all the right places. What worried M slightly was that Pastor Leakey's preaching had so far left him cold and unmoved. Many times had he felt the quivering of his spirit when certain preachers moved by the invisible power of God stirred his soul. It could be a simple inspirational message, or a theological exposition; if the speaker spoke from the heart it touched a nerve and electrified M. And in the charismatic school of Christianity to which M belonged, the ability of the speaker to move the audience was paramount to whether he became a popular speaker. A speaker able to stir the audience, either getting them crying for their sins or rocking with laughter, was sure to find willing congregations to open their ears and wallets. Walter C. Leakey was by all accounts a popular speaker; good at building the dramaturgy of his speeches, pepper them with little jokes, and finish them on an emotional note. But his affected speaking, his waving of arms, his feminine tip-toing around the stage seemed to M more like a pantomime caricature of a preacher, than a great man of God. It all seemed too stage-managed, too theatrical. Whatever Leakey spoke on he managed to make it utterly unappealing in a strange way. However true his sermon, however theologically sound his reasoning, M remained unengaged. At first M placed the fault squarely with the Pastor, as he couldn't conceive anything being the matter with himself. But after a while he doubted. Perhaps God was teaching him a lesson?

To add to the feeling of pantomime, Pastor Leakey would get one of the young male students from the Bible College to carry his huge briefcase for him. Wherever he went bouncing along, trailing behind him came a young hopeful Bible student, heavy pilot case in one hand and the pastor's change of clothes in the other, sweat pouring down his brow. This role was seen as a great boon for a young student of Christian Ministry, and there were whispers that having the strapping young lads around him, was a bit of a boon for Pastor Leakey too. These whispers were not abated by the fact that only the prettiest boys from the Bible College were selected to be the pastor's 'assistants'. More on that later.

Coming back to M now, and his vantage point of the reception view, where he found himself caught in the maelstrom of activity, in the hurricane of hectic chaos and the unthinking rush of utter busyness. He observed the frantic activity that even the vaguest of desires expressed by Leakey produced in the army of fawning sycophants that surrounded him, of which Mr Pete Crowley unbecomingly was one. It seemed strange for a large, bulldog-faced man like Mr C to be attentive and servile towards a small girlie-man like Walter Leakey. It was as unnatural as punishing the school bully by dressing him up in a pink tutu and leotards and have him serve tea and scones to the school's female staff. It would be less cruel to give him a good old-fashioned hiding, of which he could brag that he didn't cry. And so when M set about drawing a caricature of Pastor Walter and Mr C, he had all this at the back of his mind. He drew Walter Leakey walking at the front of a little procession, head high, eyes closed arrogantly, arms swinging straight out, one foot lifted with toe pointed in the above mentioned balletic fashion. Right behind him a boy is nearly breaking under the weight of two immensely heavy bags, and behind them both Mr C was drawn as an extremely fat man with short legs struggling to straddle along at the pastor's pace. Just as he had finished it one of the Brazilian pastors who worked at the church came in and M proudly showed him. He laughed and suggested M add some captions. M created a bubble with the words. "This is not good enough," going down to Walter, and, "don't worry Walter, my boys will sort it out," going to Mr C.

M then fixed it to the notice board next to his desk in the reception. A few co-workers saw it. Some laughed, some smiled insecurely, one even said: "They may not like it".

M could not imagine anyone – apart from the most tender hearted, thin-skinned... – would object to having his caricature drawn by *him*. M kept on answering calls, casting admiring glances up at his own work of art. Then the elusive and constantly unsmiling Arthur Kentworthy, Executive Assistant to the Senior Pastor, suddenly popped in – something he very seldom did. As a matter of fact M hardly ever saw him. He would come jogging in in the morning, shower, and leave late clutching a sports holdall.

Kentworthy was a sort of ominous presence. Although he was hardly ever seen, and his door always shut, he seemed to know everything that was going on in the church, and was the pastor's enforcer. Arthur Kentworthy moved with the speed and silence of a hunting cat, so M did not notice him until he was standing above him. He was looking blankly at the drawing.

"I wouldn't have that there if I were you," he said dryly before disappearing as quickly as he had come.

M felt his heart sink like a cold stone. The second most powerful man in the organisation, the second to none other than Pastor Leakey himself had disapproved. And in a most abrupt and cold manner. How dared he dislike M's drawing? Only the most tightarsed of asses could not see the excellent humour! M nevertheless thought it judicious to take the drawing down, and put it in his drawer. A few minutes later, around the corner of the corridor unto which M had direct view, came Mr C stomping like a she-rhino on the attack to protect her tots, a cloud of dust seeming to rise behind him. He barged into the reception area and looked around, putting M in mind of a bulldog sniffing for his prey.

"Where is it!" he barked.

"Not there", M reassured, pointing to the notice board.

"Well, where is it now?"

M pointed to the drawer, silently cursing himself for not having destroyed it, or hid it on his person.

"May I have it please?" Mr C ordered. M handed it over. A little later he received a call from Tracey, asking him to attend a meeting in Mr C's office. M went down the long corridor, past the Senior Pastor's office, past the Executive Assistant's office, past the pastoral office, past the music office, past the finance office, past the cell-group office, past the kitchen, pass the lavatories, until finally he turned right, then left into the ante-room where Mr C's PA Tina sat. She told M to go right in, so M knocked timidly on the door.

"Come in!" shouted Mr C and M entered. Robert Teethall, the church's Pinocchio-thin administrator was already there, so was Tracey, the reception supervisor.

"Oh dear, this *is* serious" thought M, and his mind raced to find ways in which he could deflect the lightning. One vacant chair was waiting for him, and Mr C ordered him to sit. He sat. For what seemed several minutes Mr C just stared at M with his cold blue eyes under a massive forehead. M thought he could notice just the trace of a smile at the side of his downturned mouth. Mr C held the piece of paper. Teethall shifted uneasily on his chair.

"I don't know *what* you were thinking when you hung this up on the reception wall! One thing is to draw it, but to hang it up where visitors are coming, for all to see it?!" Mr C paused.

"I am very sorry that I hung it up, I shouldn't have listened to that suggestion (*showing remorse, deflecting blame*). But, I want you to know, I only draw people that I have a real affection for (*not entirely true, but flattery often works*) and then when I showed it to Pastor Pereira he laughed and suggested I add the caption (*concretising the blame-deflection*). I would not have put it there at all if I had any idea it might be taken in the wrong way, but since he and others seemed to find it funny, I didn't think it unsuitable (*not quite true, but underlining blame deflection whilst appearing to take responsibility*). I planned to give it to Pastor Walter (*absolutely not true but makes the point of not having realised it might be offensive*). Many other staff-members saw it and thought it was funny (*true and underlining that others did not see it as offensive either*) but as soon as Mr Kentworthy said it was a bad idea to have it there I took it down (*true and showing the willingness to admit and correct mistake*)."

The little speech seemed to abate some of Mr C's disapprobation. He smiled almost perceptively now.

"You should know I was about to tell you to take your hat 'n coat! But the moment I mentioned it to Mr T and Tracey here, they (he motioned to them) protested vehemently. They went pale! They think you've done such a fantastic job on that reception they don't want to lose you. So you can thank them that you are still employed."

"Yes sir, I am terribly sorry. Obviously I won't do anything like that again."

"Pastor Pereira, you said?" Mr C said as he leaned back in his high back leather chair.

"Yes Mr C."

They all nodded knowingly, as if to say that Brazilian Pereira was a bit of a joker and he could easily lead a naïve, fresh-boy astray.

M came out from the meeting feeling rather good. He had learned that he was such a desirable employee that even a serious gaffe could not get him fired. Mr C seemed to be very much like M's own father: blustering, barking, but in essence a bit of a softie.

My son, despise not the chastening of the Lord;
neither be weary of his correction:
for whom the Lord loveth he correcteth;
even as a father the son in whom he delighteth.
PROVERBS, III; 11 – 13

CHAPTER VI

In which our hero tries to communicate and we are introduced
to the Bible Institute.

In the course of the next months M fell into a routine; travel to the Bible College in the morning, attend lectures, work upstairs in the reception in the afternoon, then in the evening it was either a church service or home to read. Some mornings he would catch a ride with Nigel, a large Zimbabwean with an old banger of a car. It was from Nigel he learned African Racialism. M had inadvertently called Nigel 'black', and was firmly and didactically disowned of the notion that all non-white, non-Arab, non-Asian Africans were 'black'. Nigel explained there are many hues, such as brown, beige, dark brown, etcetera. He regarded himself as brown, not black, because his skin was not quite as dark, and his features were less non-white. M wondered if the nuance of brownness was as important for the darkest browns, and he thought of Georg who in summer would turn as red as a boiled tomato after only the slightest exposure to the ultra-violets. He recalled the Wild West comics he used to read as a child with their terminology of redskins and palefaces. For M, the British obsession with class, and the African obsession with colour were equally useless and comical anachronisms for pre-judging an individual.

Back in his hometown people still said 'negro'. M had thought it was more politically correct to say 'coloured', but had learned that was wrong and one should say 'black', although Americans said 'African-American'. Now Nigel had told him off for saying 'black', so where does that leave one thought M?

"Hereafter I shall say *of African descent*. They can't fault me on that."

The Bible Institute was a truly multi-cultural establishment. In addition to Nigel's Zimbabwe, South Africa, France, Germany, Kenya, The Caribbean, Brazil, South Korea, Finland, Sweden, and many other nations besides, were represented. There were even a few Brits; among them Wilfred, a half-Austrian bodybuilder. Over six feet tall, blond and with a voice so boyish it seemed unbroken, he went in for a lot of hugging and lifting (preferring to lift the other boys), and had exceptionally smelly feet. Then there was Bob, a sensitive young man who also went in for hugging, and was lifted by Wilfred a lot. There was a cobble of young black ladies from the East End who gave the impression of being rather poor, and very grateful for being there. Another six-footer was Sara Grühn, a black haired German who was in charge of the Bookshop and had been 'encouraged' by the leadership of the church to attend the Bible Institute (it was an unwritten requirement for employment). And not least: a small delegation of South Koreans adorned the same four seats every morning at exactly the same time. That is, three at the same time, one always a little too late. This was Kim. M liked Kim. He had a perpetual smile on his face, a jolly, trouble-free air about him, coupled with the respectfulness of the Asian culture. He lived not far from M, and like Nigel he also had a car, so M regarded him as a bit of an asset. Communicating with him was a bit of a challenge though. Kim had an accent that went beyond parody. Firstly he refused to say 'r' where they were supposed to be, and to insert them were they did not belong. Thus he came from 'Sour Kolleeah', and when in casual conversation M asked if he liked spaghetti, he replied:

"Yes I am".

Still, M was unprepared when one early morning he heard on the radio that a planned strike by the tube workers was going ahead.

"Bloody unions," thought M as he dialled Kim's number with one hand, and stirred his cup with unspeakably strong instant coffee with the other. A pensive female voice came on the other end, almost inaudible:

"Harro?"

"Oh hello. Sorry to call so early. My name is M, I go to the Chelsea Chapel Bible Institute with Kim. Is he there?"

Silence. Some distant voices could be heard in the receiver.

Another wary voice;

"Eh, harro?"

M recognised Kim's voice.

"Ah Kim, good morning, it's M here, from Bible College".

"Oooh, M! He-he-he, good-a-molnee!"

"Yeah, good morning, but could've been better. You know there's a strike on today?"

"Stlike?"

M took another sip of the steaming black brew and drew his breath.

"Yes, the London Transport workers. They are striking. You know, not working, refusing."

"Aw, stlike! Oh, velly bad, stlike!" said Kim, as if repeating a forbidden word (which it probably was in South-Korea, imagined M).

"Yes, so NO TRAINS," M tried to keep it simple. "So I was just wondering, you know, if at all it would be possible to catch a ride with you this morning, in your car, to the Bible Institute".

"Aaawrh! But is noh potti-bell"

"Sorry?"

"Is noh potti-bell, today I go srow, he-he!"

"Oh you mean it's not possible." M wondered what he meant with going slowly.

"Is something wrong with the engine?"

"Nooo?" answered Kim puzzled. "Todah I plomised somebody I go srow."

M took another sip of coffee.

"Sorry, you promised somebody you would go *slow*?"

"Yeees, yeees! I plomised I go srow!"

M shook his head in disbelief. Truly Kim was a bit of a character, a fun loving sort of chap. But to promise somebody to go slowly didn't seem to M the nadir of hilarity, especially not at seven in the morning. Perhaps it was a bet he had lost.

"So why Kim? Why did you promise somebody to go slow?"

"Dey pay, I goh srow".

"So, was it some sort of a bet?"

"Huh? Bat? He-he, I noh know! Dey pay. Dey goh srow, dey pay me take dem."

Perhaps it was the strong coffee, or perhaps just the morning sunlight seeping through the net curtains, but slowly the mist started to lift from M's morning-dense head.

"Aah. You are taking someone to *Slough*!" M over-pronounced the name to make a point.

"Yeees, yeees! I go Srouwgh. Dey pay, I goh, he-he-he."

M said goodbye, then dialled Nigel's number, and after a trouble-free conversation secured transport. The two had a good laugh at Kim's expense as M retold the conversation.

This is the day which the Lord hath made;
we will rejoice and be glad in it.
Psalm 118; 24

As the school year wore on, M felt increasingly alienated by the revivalist-meeting style in which Mr Ralph Henderson-Bosh conducted the Bible College. There were many services you could go to if you wanted to sing hymns and jump up and down with righteous fervour. But to M it was deeply irritating that time was taken out of what ought to have been studies for which the students were paying, in order to confirm Ralph Henderson-Bosh's worldview of himself as God's gift to the church (quite literally). Gradually M began refusing to stand up when Henderson-Bosh asked everybody to stand to pray or sing or praise God (or all of the above). He would demonstrably sit with a cup of coffee, disconnecting himself from the eagerness of the occasion, observing and registering.

He saw the camp German and the tortured way in which he had to dress up his homosexuality as 'brotherly' affectionate horseplay; leading to lots of un-British hugging. Everybody hugged a lot. Framed in the rather scruffy, makeshift interior of the lecture hall, the whole Bible College took on the appearance of a field hospital where soldiers came not so much to be healed as to be patched up amidst the chaos of war. But these soldiers were not having their guts ripped apart by enemy shelling; they were having their souls and spirits shredded by the power-hungry brethren who elevate themselves into positions of power over people's fates.

They assume the role of spiritual leader and torture their flock, whipping them with guilt, feeding them scraps of conditional love before tearing them open with the bayonet of accusation, when the sought after 'revival' fails to come yet again. Students would sink down on their knees in intercessory prayer for the unsaved hell-bound world, and break down under the weight of the knowledge of their own shortcomings and the guilt for not trusting God enough. Again and again their feeling of self-worth and dignity were trampled until the leaders could take the battered shells that remained and fill it with the certainty of the leader's absolute authority.

God resisteth the proud,
but giveth grace unto the humble.
JAMES IV; 6

And the foremost spirit-crusher was Ralph Henderson-Bosh, the so-called Dean of Students. A tall, uneducated man who craved the adoring of others and preyed on the weakness of those left in his care. He was of a mixed race background and questionable family origin (which he made much of in his speeches). He had been adopted by the family who gave him the double-barrelled 'nomen', and spent much of his lectures deriding and rubbishing them in a spirit of loathing and self-pity, with which he earned himself much sympathy from some of his female pupils. With his tallness and revivalist demeanour he had an easy time pushing to one side the highly educated Headmaster of the Bible Institute, the small, skinny Mr Tim Harpier, Bachelor of Arts, Master of Theology. The son of a priest, a Greek scholar, and mild-mannered, his cerebral style did not go down very well with many of the Bible College pupils, who craved entertainment from their preachers. M had taken an immediate liking to Mr Harpier, and his impression had solidified to true love when he heard him speak in well-modulated 'received pronunciation', even tempered, articulate, intelligent; packed with knowledge and understanding. Even so, M sensed that Harpier had to dumb it down to speak to any audience, not least the current intake of the Bible Institute. But even after dumbing down he sounded thrice as intelligent as any of the other speakers M had heard so far in the Chelsea Chapel. When Harpier announced he would be giving lessons in ancient Greek, M was the first of the few who signed up, and the only one who stayed the course. M noticed the love of learning that permeated everything Harpier did and said, and his natural, unassuming pastoral qualities. One day M felt a hand on his shoulder. It was Harpier.

"Hi M, how are you? Are you learning the ropes?"

"The ropes?" replied M puzzled.

Harpier smiled. "Yes, it's an English expression. It means getting into things, learning and getting to grips with it. From the sailboat days, you understand. The ropes..."

He made a movement with both hands indicating doing something with ropes.

"Oh yes! I see. thank you Tim," M beamed and relished this scrap bit of knowledge, like a child who had just unexpectantly found a chocolate in a kitchen drawer. Harpier had obviously read him well enough to understand M would appreciate it, and as a true pastor showed his concern at the same time. M couldn't help feeling that as long as Harpier was around, everything would be all right. But as the months passed, M observed with growing concern a harried look increasingly coming over Harpier. He seemed embarrassed that he didn't have the charismatic flair of Ralph Henderson-Bosh when speaking publicly, whilst the academic nourishment he could provide was not welcomed. Like M, Harpier saw the lunacy in the frantic prayer-sessions that Ralph Henderson-Bosh whipped up with his witch-doctor qualities, but he was too cowered by his own lack of persuasion, that he daren't declare what some called 'revival', as simply emotional froth.

He kept quiet also because, just like many of the young impressionable people who sat under Ralph Henderson-Bosh, he thought perhaps something was wrong with *him*. He knew one thing was wrong: he was too white. M knew something was wrong with *them*. Still he couldn't be quite sure. God could be teaching him a new lesson. 'It must be', thought M. 'God is shedding light on another side of Christian ministry, on another nuance of the truth that I need to understand. I must be humble'. M didn't do humble very well. He was not used to self-doubt. It made him uneasy.

The Lord is nigh unto them that are of a broken heart;
and saveth such as be of a contrite spirit.
PSALM 34; 18

CHAPTER VII

In which our hero takes an initiative and coffee

M had come to respect Pete Crowley. Despite (or perhaps because of) the near sacking over the cartoons M had acted towards him in the same friendly and polite way after the incident as before it, with a beaming American-style smile and a cheerful 'good morning' or 'good afternoon' whenever Pete came by reception. Some time after the cartoon-incident Pete came by and sat down in one of the guest chairs. After chatting a little while about this and that, he said, "Although I gave you a pretty harsh time over those drawings and very nearly kicked your backside, you haven't changed your manners towards me. You don't seem offended or sore. We had it out and were finished with it. I like that."

M felt a warm glow of satisfaction for having achieved this. Oh, he could harbour a grudge if he felt unfairly treated. But a fair punishment had to be taken on the chin. He remembered the only time he'd had a proper hiding from his father. M was seven or eight and home alone for a little while. He took a kitchen knife and tried to improve the wallpaper in the hall by cutting long, deep slashes in it. Unfortunately his parents arrived just as he was finishing this artistic work, and his father did not appreciate this avant-gardist approach to home decoration. M had stubbornly refused to regret or apologise, so an old-fashion spanking of the rear was the only way. The pain brought the tears, and with the tears the catharsis. It seemed to have pained his father more; the session ended quickly once the tears and confession was done. What M remembered more than anything was the look of sadness on his father's face, it was that look that made him resolve never to do such a thing again, far more than the physical pain of the spanking. M learned that a fair-minded person must give just punishment, even it causes him agony, which can only be reduced by seeing the object of punishment taking it understandingly. This is also part of being a *man*. Now M recognised that he had made it easier for Pete by his consistency of manners, and thus Pete was due to be touched for a bit of payback. M shared his ideas for reorganisation of the reception area and improving the efficiency of post-distribution.

"Do it!" was Pete's short answer before waddling back to his suite of offices.

When Tracey Chang returned M told her, "Oh Tracey, Mr C was here and I spoke to him about some ideas of mine for changing things around a little bit".

"Did you?" said Tracey, with no apparent change in her expression.

"Yes, he said he wanted me to try and improve the appearance of the reception and the efficiency of post distribution."

"Well, you had better do it then, *isn't it?*"

It was one of Tracey's linguistic peculiarities that she inserted certain expressions that didn't quite fit the idiom. Another was to say "ta" when "thank you" had been more appropriate. Tracey was probably irritated by M going above her head like he had, but it could not be learned from looking at her dead-pan face. To M, Tracey seemed like some humanoid Asian robot; she just went around functioning with perfect deference to her superiors and exact correctness to her peers and subordinates. But surely underneath that smooth surface emotions computed and sent signals back and forth inside her soybean fired brain. M took great pleasure in reorganising the reception area. He moved the filing cabinet used for the staff's mail and the franking machine, into the packing-room next to reception, along with the post-bags for outgoing mail. This freed up area in reception to create a more comfortable and tidy-looking visitors' area. M's first little reform had been executed and as he surveyed the result he felt immensely satisfied. All subsequent initiatives would be carried out with the same boundless confidence in his own judgment.

his book of the law shall not depart out of thy mouth; but thou shalt meditate therein day and night, that thou mayest observe to do according to all that is written therein: for then thou shalt make thy way prosperous, and then thou shalt have good success.
THE BOOK OF JOSHUA I; 8

A special staff meeting was called. From across the organisation employees were called, and came looking slightly bedraggled as they shook off the wetness of the autumnal rain. M was asked to close reception, which was not usual; so it had to be something serious, M thought. After prayers performed by Charlie Hatkinson, with perfect consideration for coiffure, senior pastor Walter Leakey stood up before his staff.

"Satan wears many disguises," he started. "One of the more subtle expressions of Satanic qualities is *presumption*. Presumption can sneak in through many little cracks and crevices. Presuming one is saved on the back of religious ritual. Presuming one is anointed without grace or healed without God's personal interjection. Taking God as a slot machine where you put in a coin, pull the arm and out comes the answer *you* want. Presuming to know better than God."

To M these comments sounded strange. He saw Christianity as a renewal of the legalistic, contractual relationship between the Hebrews and their God. Through the sacrifice of Jesus Christ our side of the contract had been fulfilled, our liabilities cancelled and every promise ever given to His people extended to those who became born-again by the spirit; becoming rightful claimants to the Abrahamic blessings by *faith*, not *deeds*. The very essence of Martin Luther's struggle was the rediscovery of the value the early Christian church put on pure faith as the requirement for salvation. M's own journey into Christianity had been through the understanding that it was not about becoming embroiled in strange rituals and a religious demeanour; it was simply about believing in Christ, and by that one was let off the hook. The healing of infirmities, the provision of material needs, the blessing upon work we undertake; all this was in the Hebrew contract, if they kept their part of the bargain. The whole point of Christianity was that Christ had fulfilled God's Law perfectly, and by accepting Him as one's Lord and Saviour one was automatically granted all these blessings.

Christ hath redeemed us from the curse of the law, being made a
curse for us: for it is written, Cursed is every one that
hangeth on a tree:
that the blessing of Abraham might come on the Gentiles through
Jesus Christ; that we might receive the promise of the Spirit
through faith.
GALATIANS III; 13 – 14

Was it suddenly presumptuous to believe that God's blessings belonged to one? That healing and prosperity had been promised? Was it suddenly down to our deeds after all? Were we no better than the Catholics? Pastor Leakey went on:

"If we take God's grace as an excuse for our lack of action, or if we think God can be compelled by us, we are heading down a very dangerous route. On the other hand, if we think that by taking action we can make God respond in a certain way, we are equally wrong".

"Well, this *is* a lose-lose situation then," thought M. "We cannot get what we want from God by grace alone – that would be lazy, and we mustn't think it helps to do anything either – that would be presumption. The long and the short of this matter is that we must struggle on, but not expect any help from God. He may help. But then again, he may not. We must simply hope to be doing His will, so that he might bless us in unexpected ways. That is always the excuse for the disappointed, with unanswered prayers and unpaid bills. The single mother who gave the last few pounds she had in the collection and now hasn't the money to pay for her child's school lunches. Or the parents worried sick about their son's drug abuse. Don't worry, God will bless you in ways you don't know. Did your son die from an overdose? Well, perhaps it was for the best, in a way we cannot see now. But how can you count your blessings if you don't even know what they are?" This was not the Christianity M believed in. It was everything he despised and disliked about religion.

Leakey was coming to a point:

"As you all know, we published my new book before the summer. For sales this was not an ideal time, but we took a leap of faith. Up to now we have not sold the expected number of copies. In fact, we have sold so few that we have a serious shortfall in the cash flow. If we don't start shifting those books there is the real possibility that we shan't be able to pay out the salaries on time".

A sombre look descended on the faces of all present. People were uncomfortable, but didn't want to show any sign of doubting the providence of the Lord, or give any outward signs of not *walking in faith*. So they simply assumed a serious, earnest, slightly glum appearance, as the images of unpaid invoices flashed before their eyes. Mr Kentworthy sat bold upright, Charlie Hatkinson slouched, trying to appear relaxed. Leakey continued:

"In order for us to make sure we have the cash flow needed we must all do our bit."

He went on to present a plan that would turn every staff-member into booksellers. Those staff-members who were in charge of satellite churches would be given a quota to sell, either directly or through their underlings, who in turn would do the same down the line in a sort of blessed pyramid scheme, but without the promise of getting rich quick. Just the hope you might be paid your salary. Other staff would be given various timeslots and places to stand, where they would push the books on the churchgoers before and after services. The church's bookshop would only promote this book, and from the pulpit this book would be flogged in every service until they had sold enough.

At the very next service Pastor Leakey took the stage and declared he had been, "moved by God," because this book contained a special blessing that would prove a breakthrough in people's life, and that Satan was trying to keep the blessings from them. Even M proved not to be completely immune to this narrative, and when Leakey decided to start putting small, anointed prayer-cloths inside the sleeve of books, M was caught up in the naïve excitement of it all. He failed to see the Catholic implication of the small cloths, and he forgot the principle so central to his belief: by faith *alone*. Being quite the salesman M threw himself into the hawking of books with great alacrity, and managed to shift quite a few of them. Very soon he started receiving appreciative, knowing nods from Pastor Leakey, whilst Pete Crowley looked at him with something akin to fatherly pride.

Between services M would often take coffee in one of Chelsea's many coffee shops. This Sunday, after a particularly successful bout of book selling, he spotted

Peter Carrington with the rather downcast air of a drenched cat. M invited him along for coffee, which seemed to cheer him up a bit. Peter was in his early forties. Dark blond floppy hair, blue eyes and an aristocratic demeanour that was a cross between Peter O'Toole's Lawrence and Sebastian from *Brideshead*. M liked Peter. He was one of the few true *English*men in the church, and an upper class one at that. Always with a certain savoir-vivre, he would saunter into a room with a careless sharpness of observation that took the trivial seriously and treated the serious with the greatest triviality. There was an effeminacy in his movements that suited his having a theatrical background, and a pleasant fluidity in his tenor voice that could never satiate M.

Peter was in charge of the School of Creative Ministry, a sub-division of the Bible College close to the former ballet dancer Walter Leakey's heart, but by his carefree attitude one could not detect the slightest hint of the responsibility that laid on him, nor the great care which he did have for his students. Unlike the many who need to show the weight of their worries, Peter never let on. He had a mocking lightness about him, always sparring wits with M or Mr C, or anyone else he deemed his peer. Those not his peer he treated with a kindly condescension bore out of a noblesse oblige not artificially assumed. Towards Walter he acted with a playful respectfulness. His large blue eyes, with a hint of sadness, would look playful, his mouth half open either humming a tune or being on the verge of saying something, his scruffy cardigan would hang down on his slender frame, his arms would wave through the air as he took in the scent and delivered a pertinent sarcasm. It was therefore all the more out of character that his eyes suddenly had more of the sadness and less of the playfulness. It was, thought M, a bit like picking up a book you've read before and find the words had changed.

They sat down in the farthest corner of the café, with a large cup each, and after a few moments of quiet coffee sipping M broke the pauciloquence:

"Peter... you seem rather ... thoughtful today."

Peter continued to stare into his latte.

"Hm! Yes, well…" He lifted his head, leaned back in the easy chair, and smiled one of his resigned smiles.

"What do you think about us possibly not being paid at the end of the month?" Peter said it with an unusually earnest look on his face.

The weight of the statement took M by surprise, coming from Peter. The lack of irony was slightly troubling, but liberating at the same time.

"Well I… I thought… I mean I think... it is quite…" M shook his head ever so slightly. Peter took it as confirmation.

"Hm, indeed. You see, this isn't the first time." He said it with the air of the conspirator.

"No?" M was genuinely surprised at this.

Peter shook his head slowly.

"Oh no. A few years back Walter pushed for a gargantuan conference to be put on in Wembley Arena. The church had to pay up-front fees to reserve the Arena, and what with that and all the other expenses we were simply told that either we shift tickets, or we don't get paid. Now, is that *right*? Is that how it *should* be?"

Peter looked searchingly at M with his big, blue, sad boy's eyes.

M shifted uncomfortably in his chair.

"Well it's…certainly not pleasant," he said diplomatically.

M didn't *do* disloyal, but Peter's words had struck a chord with him, and he wanted Peter to know that he understood and agreed, without sounding too critical of the spiritual leadership; there was a hint of sinfulness in being too critical. Peter continued to talk about the conference, the way it was presented as a challenge from God, and how they had to rise to this and take 'steps in faith' in order for God's blessings to be released. In the end the salaries had come through, so perhaps that proved God *had* blessed it. Still, it had been tough on the nerves of all those working in the church with mortgages and rents to pay. Was it justifiable?

M never like whinging. He didn't like complainers, moaners, groaners and faultfinders. People, frozen in the headlight of their own fear of failure, arrested in their spiritual development because they are so afeard of making a slight slip-up, they'd much rather lean back and criticise those who at least do *something*.

If people didn't even have faith the size of a mustard seed, they had better get the hell out (so to speak) of the church business. But although that was his default setting, he couldn't help but understand Peter's point. Staff took up financial liabilities in the trust that the church's finances would be subject to good, sensible husbandry. And then comes along an arm-waving, failed ballet dancer and demands to be centre stage at Wembley Arena at excruciating costs to all but himself. And this was the crux of the matter: M knew something was seriously wrong with Walter. He tried to suppress the notion, but as with his father before him, M had a near unshakable confidence in his own judgment. As the two men leaned back in their chairs sipping their coffee silently, M thought of his dad.

And Jesus said unto them... for verily I say
unto this mountain, Remove hence to yonder place; and it shall
remove: and nothing shall be impossible unto you.
Matthew XVII; 20

"Well you know Peter, I think we must simply choose not to worry. The Lord is in control somehow," M said with a forced positivity.

Peter nodded but looked sadly disappointed, as if M had dropped down a few notches in his estimation. M noticed it and regretted immediately what he had said.

"What I mean Peter is... what other options do we have? We're in the church business. The show must go on and all that! Walter must act on his vision, mustn't he? If we don't agree with him we can quit. But at the end of the day, *he* is the pastor, *he* is the leader, and we, if we think he is doing what God wants him to do, must follow."

M thought he had delivered a good, logical case for the defence, but felt strangely sullied and dissatisfied by it never the less.

Peter smiled with his mouth and looked at M sadly: "Of course M, you're quite right."

CHAPTER VIII

In which we meet the Finnish caretaker and
our hero smells the odour of sin

As it happened the salaries did come through that month, and M had done such a fine job shifting books that he had earned himself a few brownie points in the eyes of the senior leadership, not least in Pete's. Increasingly Pete used to come and sit on one of the guest chairs in the revamped reception and have little chats with M, before waddling back. At first M was surprised that the church's second in command should find the time to sit with a lowly receptionist. But he realised that Pete liked him and he decided to make the most of it. One day as Pete sat and waited for M to finish with a caller M thought he would try his luck. As he finished the call he turned to Pete and said, "Pete, I am soon finished with my year in the Bible Institute. I don't think I will be doing the second year, and so I need to find some more work. Are there any full time vacancies in the church?"

Pete leaned back and crossed his arms. With a frown he said, "And why do you want to work full time for the church?"

M looked at him steadily, knowing full well that any hyper-spiritual talk of wanting to give one's life to the service of the heavenly kingdom would not wash with this man.

"I want to earn some more money, so I can get a better place to live. My current flat is a dump, and I want to get a decent place. Something I can call *home*".

Pete chuckled. "I am glad you said that. I had half feared you would break into a rousing speech on building the House of the Lord etcetera. But that's what I like about you M: you're down to earth. You're not flaky", he illustrated flakiness by holding the palm of his hand out wobbling it. "You gave me your ambition to better yourself as reason, and that, in my book, is a good reason."

M felt a slight need to say something to increase his spiritual credential, and perhaps sensing this, Pete continued, this time holding his palm up defensively:

"I know you are as spiritual as any of them – probably more – but there are a lot of flakes out there, who will *hallelujah* to your face and shout and dance and shanday-moranday," he was wobbling his hand again, "but at the first smell of trouble they shoot off like rats from a sinking ship".

M sensed a tinge of bitterness in Pete's words.

"All right M. Don't worry, I will have a talk with Walter and see what we can do".

He rose, grunting as he did, and struggled back to his office. M felt a tingling of excited anticipation.

During the term break M was asked to help out as a caretaker half the day, and to continue as a receptionist the other half. M saw it as a test from Pete and gladly accepted, finding himself reporting to the Finnish head-caretakeress Ellina. Ellina was a formidable female. A cross between Pippi Longstocking and Hulk Hogan, she had in her past competed professionally in weightlifting. When she girded her loins with the help of the caretaker belt, pulled her hair back and started steaming through the building, woe betide anyone who stood in her way. Lights were changed, chairs moved, floors washed in a turbo whirlwind of concentrated energy. After ploughing through the building leaving a trail of strict Finnish tidiness in her wake, she would cook herself a hearty lunch in the staff canteen, and in her thick Finnish accent rail against the untidiness of people in London or laugh loudly at her own jokes. She could be sardonically sarcastic, but did not understand irony. And any wordplay or linguistically based joke was completely lost on her without a five-minute exposition, after which she would wave it off as schoolboy silliness. She was fair-minded, no-nonsense, matter-of-fact, and utterly unsentimental.

M liked and disliked, feared and despised her in equal parts. Ellina had finished her first year at the Bible Institute as M started his first, and was now in her second year. She was only part-time employed, but being very conscientious she would work late to complete any job she had started. M's heavy-labour experience at the fishing trawler and his lavatory-washing experience in the army, now stood him in good stead as Ellina saw his presence as the chance to get all the jobs done that she hadn't been able to do on her own. The Tabernacle Hall had huge toilet areas, with ten seats in the men's and twenty in the ladies'. M washed and scrubbed and made them shine and smell fragrantly of chemical lemon.

Ellina came in and stood, boots apart, hands on hips, like a sergeant major. She sniffed, then had a look around in all nooks and crannies, inspected the washbasins and the mirrors and to M's great relief smiled ever so slightly and said: "verry kood M. Verry kood".

Then, inspection over, she marched out. M would realise that from the Finn, this was as near ecstatic as she could get.

Around this time a new person started working for the Bible Institute, as admin assistant. His name was Isaac Gomez, and just like Paddington Bear he was from the darkest Peru. His skin had the colour of creamy cocoa, his hair coffee, and his face was smooth and beardless. Isaac was seventeen, had just arrived in Britain with his mother, and his work in the Bible Institute was on a voluntary basis, as he waited for permission to stay in the country. M was immediately struck by Isaac's prettiness. He had the most charming smile, and a longish nose on which he wore round, steel-rimmed specs through which M could see large, brown, coyly shy eyes. His thick, cherry-red lips would form into a V-shaped smile when he saw M, and he would come and sit in the reception until M could get off the phone.

"They told me in the bible college office that you could show me how to do the franking machine. They want me to do mailing," he said with a sort of smiling helplessness, like a maiden in distress that appealed to M's masculine instinct. He wanted to protect Isaac. To hold him close to himself and say, "it's alright, I won't let them send you back to Peru".

He imagined Isaac closing his eyes as he pressed his head against M's chest believing that everything would be just as M said.

"Do THE mailing" M corrected.

"THE mailing" Isaac giggled.

Then Jonathan and David made a covenant, because he
loved him as his own soul.
I Samuel XVIII; 3

M conducted Isaac into the mailroom and showed him how to set the correct postage on the franking machine, and how to print out the stickers. And as he stood next to Isaac and watched him try out the new found knowledge successfully, he couldn't resist placing his hand on Isaac's shoulder in what could simply be an encouragement, pressing him gently towards himself whilst saying, "yeah, that's it. Well done!" Then, what M shouldn't want but did want, happened, as Isaac, rather than resisting M's slight tugging, pressed himself against M and inclined his head onto M's shoulder as he said in a breathy voice "thank you M".

As in slow motion M let his hand slip down Isaac's back, just touching his buttocks slightly in passing. No reaction. Isaac stood too still, as if waiting for something. M saw his hand being raised slowly towards Isaac's buttocks again, this time touching them purposely. Isaac remained still. Then he turned his head and looked up at M. M bowed his head to kiss his cheek but Isaac caught his mouth and they locked in a deep kiss. M held Isaac firmly as the latter fumbled his way to M's developing bulge. It was a moment that felt very long as they stood solidified in the dark, sinful sweetness of the embrace, in that tiny, stuffy post-room. M felt a mad excitement. He squeezed Isaac's buttocks and wanted to throw caution to the wind and undress there and then. Suddenly they heard the door opening and they tore apart both swirling themselves with lightning speed toward the franking machine as Steve Wagger, a chubby Texan in the Bible College's second year came crashing in.

"Hey bruther M, how 'ya doin' man? Lissen, I need to do some mailin' for the paestor's office. If I bring it down, can you show me how t' do it?"

M had half turned towards Steve, still holding his index finger on the franking machine as if pointing something out to Isaac. "Why, yes of course Steve. Just bring it down when it's ready and I'll show you", he said smiling brightly.

"Awrighdy then, see you in a liddle while".

He turned around on his heels and shot back to where he had come from.

"Do you think he saw us?" Isaac said worriedly.

"No chance" said M. "Steve is not very observant anyway. Don't you worry."

"What did we just do M?" said Isaac. "What happened there?"

M's guiltless Christianity came in handy now.

"It is quite natural Isaac. This is a physical thing; it happens. God created sexuality, and we need to control it. We didn't and so that is a sin, but there is forgiveness for sin. Let's go into Tracey's office and pray".

He led his little friend into Tracey's empty office. They closed the door and got on their knees. M knew one didn't have to get on one's knees, but thought perhaps the Catholic influence of Isaac's South American upbringing would make him more comfortable if some degree of ritualistic religiosity was displayed.

"Dear Lord," M prayed, "you see and know everything, and so we simply bow before you now and confess that we have both sinned against your will, and let you down. You see our hearts and so you know we regret it. We choose to repent and turn away from that sinful way, and to submit ourselves to your will. We thank you that the blood of Jesus has washed away all sin and the consequences of it, and we also know that your word says that if we confess our sin and turn away from it, it *is* forgiven. We thank you for making us new creatures in Christ Jesus, and for giving us strength through your spirit to live according to your will, every day, in Jesus' name, amen!"

M looked at Isaac who looked less devoted to the prayer than M had expected. "Yes, that felt genuine" was all he said, and M was glad he felt so.

If we confess our sins, he is faithful and just to forgive us
our sins, and to cleanse us from all
unrighteousness.
THE FIRST EPISTLE GENERAL OF JOHN I; 9

Isaac continued to work in the institute's admin office for a couple of months, then as suddenly as he had appeared he stopped appearing. M missed him and worried he and his family had been sent back to Peru. Suddenly he burst through the doors and came to sit on a visitor's chair. M completed the call he was on, eyes fixed on Isaac throughout, who sat with a little smile on his mouth, as if he had just stolen a cake and eaten it before it was discovered.

"Isaac, how nice to see you. I've been missing you round here. What are you doing?"

Isaac sat on his hands like a schoolboy in the head master's office.

"I have had a few things to sort out in connection with the permit. I was not even allowed to volunteer, which is why I have not been around for a while."

He looked straight at M.

"I'm eighteen now, which means I am legally no longer a minor", he smiled. "We had to move out of the flat we had, and my mother went to stay with a friend. Not really much space there…" he let the sentence hang in mid-air. M didn't need more prodding.

"Would you like to come and kip on my sofa? It's not very comfy, but at least you won't have your mother there". Isaac nodded eagerly with the cake-thief smile on his lips.

They travelled together to M's place. On the tube they stood next to each other, both holding on to the bar above. M allowed his little finger to touch Isaac's, who allowed his to be touched. A tickle went through M's body. Then on the bus M pointed to Isaac's watch, and under the pretence of wanting to inspect it, took Isaac's hand and held it. Thus they sat like two schoolboy sweethearts holding hands until they arrived at the stop. They went down to the fish and chip shop and spent the first part of the evening eating, chatting and not knowing how to proceed. It finally became time to go to bed. M's bedsit had an en suite bathroom, so M sat listening to all Isaac was doing in the bath, imagining what he looked like as he stood there. When he came out he was wearing a large T-shirt and boxer shorts. His legs were darker than M had imagined, and somewhat skinnier. M felt like a big, pale, Scandinavian whale, and decided not to stray from his habit of sleeping in flannel pyjamas. When he came out from the bath Isaac was sitting up in the sofa, covered by the quilt, reading a magazine. M went to his bed in the corner. He looked at Isaac. Then he looked at the bookshelf behind him.

"Oh, I think I would like a book to read" he said in a low voice, as to himself.

He got up and stood behind Isaac. But rather than study the row of books his attention was merely directed at Isaac's neck and his dark pink ears. He finally dared to bow down and kiss Isaac's neck. The latter turned his head and their lips met. M led him over to the bigger bed and laid him down. Isaac was pliable, willing and softly encouraging. M pulled Isaac's T-short slowly off and leaning down kissed his dark brown nipples as if they were a woman's. Isaac let out a surprised yelp of pleasure as if it had never occurred to him that this could be done. M continued down and gently pulled the boxer shorts down. His own flannels were soon clumsily torn off, and they fumbled their way to a sixty-nine position. Isaac signalled he was willing for M to enter him. M quickly ran off to the bathroom and got some moisturising cream. It would have to do, he thought, as it was all he had. He applied it, Isaac got into the correct position on all fours and M worked his way into him. It was a feeling of power and manliness to bore into the younger man, who raised his hairless torso and pressed himself against M's hairy chest. M folded his arms around him, and as Isaac leaned his head backwards unto M's shoulder, M softly inclined his head against Isaac's and they stood like that, slowly moving, melting into one another, the warm sweat of both bodies mingling; being close. M felt masterful, in masculine control. But as Isaac lowered his torso back to the forward position, a smell rose to M's nostrils that was wholly unattractive. M wondered why he had allowed himself to do this. After sex they washed, and then went back to bed. They slept naked and held each other close. M wished they could just lie like that, and never again have sex. Just the closeness, without the disgusting, revolting bodily taste. M didn't like the smell of sin.

The next morning they dressed silently and took breakfast without talking about what had happened. Isaac left, and M stood watching him from his first floor windows. Down on the sidewalk he saw a diminutive young man, making his way to the bus stop alone. M knew he didn't love him and couldn't protect him.

Love not the world, neither the things that are in the world. If any man love the world, the love of the Father is not in him. For all that is in the world, the lust of the flesh, and the lust of the eyes, and the pride of life, is not of the Father, but is of the world. And the world passeth away, and the lust thereof: but he that doeth the will of God abideth forever.
1 John II; 15 – 17

CHAPTER IX

In which our hero buys cigar and we learn Pastor Walter's big secret

It was a Saturday, so after breakfast M decided to go to town. He alighted at Bond Street Station, turned right at the Oxford Street exit and then right again down Davies Street before veering left into South Molton Lane, where he sat down outside a coffee shop with the Saturday *Times* and a cappuccino. He leafed dutifully through the paper, but was more interested in the people filing past. Occasionally he would catch a Scandinavian language being spoken loudly, as if the speakers thought nobody could understand them in London. Having finished his coffee M grew restless and carried on his perambulation down South Molton Lane turning left into Brook Street, then right into New Bond Street. He peered into the madly exclusive little jewellery shops and various fashion boutiques, went past Asprey's then turned left before Old Bond Street, then right into Burlington Arcade where he nodded to the beautifully uniformed watchman who stood elegantly enforcing the ban on running, whistling and humming. M wondered what would happen if a very fit person would run quickly through the arcade, whistling loudly before humming violently. The portly gilded guard would perchance throw off his garb and reveal a svelte physique underneath, able to swing himself from one hanging lamp to the other and catch up with the culprit before reaching Piccadilly on the other side. Then what? 'What can he actually do about it?' wondered M, before an antique wristwatch caught his attention, then another, then an antique fountain pen, then countless others. M thought this was how London ought to be. There were hardly any spottable tourists in Burlington Arcade. There were men in suits and hats, women with high hair and tasteful tweed skirts. Some older Japanese *not* wielding cameras, and a couple of badly dressed Scandinavians who had wandered in by mistake, gawping at the unfathomable old world charm that never could come flat-packed from Ikea.

He emerged into the tourist-cauldron that is Piccadilly. Italian youths shouting and gesticulating, Japanese clad in branded clothes clutching huge cameras, Americans complaining and pointing, Scandinavians hitting people with their rucksacks whenever they turned around, Germans ticking off a been-there list over official attractions. He walked quickly westward through the mass, trying to look uninterested, and crossed over Piccadilly continuing down St James' Street. On the corner of St James' and Jermyn Street he entered through a pair of glass doors, with brass handles shaped as huge pipes, and was at once inside a cigar shop where the attendants wore suits, the younger with blond, floppy hair, the elder with greying beards. M looked around slowly. They had pipes in all shapes, they had brollies and walking sticks, they had lighters and tobacco, and in the far end M spotted the cigar-room. The intensely pleasant smell of wood and tobacco lay in the room, like incense. This was holy ground. A large American couple entered. The lady pointed to a large tin sign over the tobacco shelf.

"Look Herb", she exclaimed in a loud, braying American voice, "*thank you for smoking* it says".

M turned and looked at the sign, and smiled. M's father always bought a box of cigars for Christmas. The smell conjured up for M the feeling of luxurious contentment that would hang in the air after the Christmas dinner, as the coffee, cognac and liqueurs were presented along with chocolates and various confectioneries and mixed with the expectations of the mystical presents keeping their secrets under the tree. As unwrapping unfolded, the bittersweet frankincense of cigar-smoke spread its blanket across the room, enveloping the star at the top of the Christmas tree in a blue-grey mist. The old cigar-shop at the corner of St James and Jermyn Street was a magical wardrobe through which one entered the world that once was. It was the word as it could and should be, rather than what it had ever been. For M it stirred the spirit of all he loved with the idea of the British. Phileas Fogg, Sherlock Holmes, and the writings of Kipling had been part of his growing up.

Even through his dark period of Polish films and Russian literature, he was never less interested if a British adaptation came on the telly. He devoured anything from the chocolate-box mystery of an Agatha Christie crime story to the largeness of Dickens, or the cool competence of George Smiley, via the sheer beauty of Brideshead's strange world. But Phileas Fogg occupied a special place in his heart. It celebrated something M found particularly attractive and peculiarly old-world British: relentless attention to consistency of standards. Fogg would have his tea at teatime and he would never cease being gentlemanly whatever the adversity. This, thought M, was how they came to dominate the world. If Britain had gone down in the world since the days of empire, the failure to take tea at its preordained time was symptomatic of the decline. M had never found the flower-power rejection of traditional values altogether reassuring. It seemed to him to lead to a corrosion of values, good as well as bad, of authority, good as well as the not so good, resulting in a jellyfish society where everything is equally permissible and nothing therefore matters. The 'revolutionary' ideas of the '68 generation were not much more than a regurgitation of ideas known for at least three and half millennia, from the

Greek sophists who questioned traditional mores, via the scepticism of the seventeenth century to the subjectivity of existentialism; it all seemed to boil down to the intellectual laziness of, 'it may not be true for you but it is true for me.' (Or vice versa.) Romanticism had given us the ideal of the lonesome genius, who in adversity forges new ways. This was fine when applied to Beethoven or Darwin, but when the children of chartered accountants decided that they will 'find themselves' by travelling around in a VW campervan smoking pot, the principle has deteriorated from liberty to laxity. Freedom requires self-discipline not indulgence. It demands that you face reality rather than run from it by soaking your brain in chemicals and weeds.

M laughed at those who, rejecting the suit and tie because they don't want to 'conform', run off to the fashion stores to buy the same mass-produced costumes as everyone else. Wishing to have freedom without standards we have lost both. When the line between good and bad gets smudged into an ever-expanding grey zone, who can tell what is pomposity and what is real dignity? What is straightforwardness and what is crudeness? What is acceptable openness and what is plain vulgarism? M had recently read in the paper that the new Prime Minister had abandoned formal titles around the cabinet table, and he resented it deeply.

Is it progress to call a stranger 'mate' rather than 'Sir,' or 'Johnnie' rather than 'Mr Smith'? M didn't think so, and it is always more a restraint on those in power that they have to refer to their subordinates by reference to the office or the title, than it is a liberation for the subordinate to call his superior by his first name. And so he turned around, slowly drinking in the milk of old-worldliness so lovingly preserved in this little kingdom seemingly untouched by hideous modernity. This shop did not pump out loud; thumping pop-music like the hellholes of Oxford Street, the shop assistants did not wear world-weary faces and baggy clothes. They looked like younger version of the older shop assistants. Their hair was combed and their bodies clad in blue suits. Their whole beings seemed to say, "Sir, you've come here because you like to be called 'Sir'. You've come here because you want us to be impeccably correct. You want to believe, Sir, that we are all nephews of baronets and country squires, and indeed some of us are."

"We will help you keep up the belief that standards still exist, that they never went away. That the two world wars never killed our collective faith in humankind. Sir, you are here because you reject the 'pile-'em-high-sell-'em-cheapness' of modern consumerism. These products, Sir, have taken a long time to make. They are made to exacting high standards; they are proven by time and unbroken tradition to be the best by an unchallengeable standard. You prove your good taste, Sir, by entering our little world, and it welcomes you, Sir".

His eyes rested on the polished pipes, the rows of tobacco, the hand-made lighters, the walking sticks – and oh how he wanted one – the brollies, and then his imaginary monocle fell from his eye as he fastened his gaze on the cigar-room in the corner. He floated towards it, not noticing that he came to a halt in front of the glass door, transfixed by the vision of this Aladdin's cave of cigars in such numbers and variety as he never before had seen. A man of respectable maturity, grey-streaked receding hair and neat beard, rushed quietly to the door in front of M and said quietly;

"Allow me, Sir".

Perhaps he thought M had deliberately stopped to wait for an appropriately subservient door opener to come to his aid. In this little kingdom where the oxymoron 'self-service' was not known and roles were played devotedly, M had raised the stakes by playing a role he probably could not afford. Waking up to this harsh reality he mumbled a drawling "oh, thank yew", as he just happened to pop his hand in his pocket, and proceeded to rummage around in search of hard currency. Thankfully the shelves had prices hand-written on little labels, and pretending not to notice them M quickly reckoned he could afford *one* proper Havana of the smallish variety.

"Is Sir looking for anything in particular?" the man said.

"Oh I just wanted one for after lunch", said M in a tone that he hoped would convey that he had boxes of the stuff in the cellar of his country house, but had forgotten to grab a few for his day in the city.

"Any particular favourites, Sir?"

From previous experience M could at least answer this question without hesitation or deviation.

"Oh, I think Montecristo is my favoured smoke. Rich, without being overpowering".

"Indeed, Sir", said the impeccable one, "a very popular cigar", and drew M's attention to an entire shelf stocked with varieties of said brand. M wished he had liked a less 'popular' cigar.

"Any particular size, Sir?"

Mercilessly they came to the crux of the matter.

"Well", M looked around at prices of £16, £22, £150, and tried, "Just an after lunch smoke, you understand".

"Of course, Sir. How about this?" He pointed to a shelf with the price tag '£6.50'. It was a medium smallish cigar, but crucially within M's budged. Whether the old gent had divined M's pecuniary position, or always recommended this as a lunch-smoke, M couldn't know.

"This is a lovely lunch smoke, Sir. I often take it myself…"

"Yes, yes, it looks very nice." In a moment of over-confident folly he heard himself say: "I normally smoke the bigger ones you see, but…"

"Well, we *have* bigger ones, Sir…"

"No, no, this will be perfectly fine to try. I *want* to try it." M wanted to say something that would boost his cigar aficionado credentials. He remembered something he had read.

"I understand the Americans like their cigars more humid than the British".

"That is possible, Sir, I wouldn't know".

Of course he wouldn't, why would he? M tried again: "I know some people dip the tip of their cigars in port before smoking it. Is that something you would recommend?"

At this the polite one drew up a little, and said slowly:

"Only, Sir, if you have a very poor cigar, or a very poor port" (and then turning to look at M) "or *both*".

M did not feel the need to relay the fact that he had tried this abomination. The courteously delivered yet robust response was a far cry from the 'if it works for you', and it left M feeling clean and clear and happy, which was more than he had felt the evening before with Isaac. He took his precious specimen to a coffee shop in Jermyn Street where he could sit in the back yard and drink coffee, read another paper, and soak himself in the cigar fumes.

As he smoked, M reflected on what had happened between him and Isaac. It would have been the expected thing to go for counselling after falling so thoroughly into sin, but M simply didn't feel the need to be told by a pastor what he already knew: that although the spirit is born again and willing, the flesh is weak and still drawn to sin, that we must keep it in check, but when we fail there is forgiveness through the blood of Christ. One might think that pastors are pleased with low maintenance sheep in the flock, such as M. Not so. Pastors are like flies, drawn to the shitty side of human nature. They need the 'needy'. It's what keeps them employed and gives them their raison d'etre.

Just as a car mechanic in a world of perfect cars would be superfluous, a pastor would have no place in a church of self-preserving worshippers. But the combination of impossible demands and conflicting theologies keep scores of believers guilty and confused, and thus in need of the counsel of pastors. M had had a peculiar spiritual upbringing with Sigmund in Norway. Sigmund was not a typical pastor; he was not as interested in humans' failing as in humans' successes. Norwegian Christianity, on the windswept, rocky west coast of this little nation, was permeated by a gloomy, unrelenting, puritan pietism. For generations of strugglers, eking out a meagre living off the rough sea or barren land, the low-church devotion to a just provider created a framework of quiet, serious purposefulness in the largely joyless, disciplined lives of the small communities. It was a form of Christianity that seemed utterly unappealing to M.

In sharp contrast to this, Sigmund Fjeld's church was an explosion of joy, fun, noise and positivity. Sigmund had imported an American guiltless Christianity. A Christianity that is in part religion, in part motivational course for self-improvement for the success God wants you to enjoy. In this Christianity material wealth was not only permissible, but desirable, as a sign of God's blessing. In this Christianity you were not merely a forgiven sinner struggling to reform, but a born-again conqueror destined to win. The preachers in this vein of the Christian faith did not have serious, frowning faces, heavy with the guilt and short-comings of human depravity, but big, shiny, white toothy smiles and beaming eyes topped by a perfectly coiffed head of hair. They wore expensive suits and jewellery and flew private jets. Pastor Sigmund was not like other pastors; he genuinely appreciated the low-maintenance, self-preserving succeeding sheep. M had up to the time he came to Chelsea Chapel assumed that was how all successful churches were. He had not realised that the spirit of dark puritanism hung over most of European evangelical Christianity, including the London church. It was *his* and Sigmund's Christianity that was the exception, the un-normal, the marginal.

The Reverend Pastor Walter Leakey might have liked M better if he had come to him with his little problem. But M seemed far too self-preserved to

Walter. M had never come to Walter with any problem or frustration, any failing or any shortcoming, which would have enabled Walter to grant him gladness of heart by pouring over him pity and big-heartedness. It was the way he, and most pastors, operated; get to know your subjects' weaknesses, their sins and faults, and then use it as a spiritual crowbar to prise open their soul – the relationship being one of mutual dependence. It is the reason why so many pastors end up surrounded by flawed characters. The flawed ones need the pastor's graceful tolerance, his help in 'dealing' with the issues, and the pastor needs the flawed ones to have someone to shine a kindly face of patient forbearance on. But if M didn't ask for it, Walter could not grant it.

Walter had wanted M to come and work for him. But M wasn't like the other young lads in the Bible College who would come up and swarm around Walter whenever he was in their midst. He had felt snubbed by M, and instead his eye had been fixed upon a young Danish man, nineteen summers young, with thick, wavy, blond hair and stunningly blue eyes. Frederic had asked to see Walter privately for 'counselling', and had confessed to the sin of homosexuality.

Thou shalt not lie with mankind, as with womankind:
it is abomination.
Neither shalt thou lie with any beast to defile thyself therewith:
neither shall any woman stand before a beast to lie down thereto:
it is confusion.
Defile not ye yourselves in any of these things
LEVITICUS XVIII; 22 – 24

Immediately Walter had been able to grant him some peace of heart. This, explained Walter, was only a sin if acted on, and that God would be able to heal him completely, that God loved him just as much as He otherwise would, and that in order for Frederic to learn to control his emotions and focus on the service of God, he would be allowed to come and have some salaried ministry-experience in the Senior Minister's office. Fred could not believe his luck. Not only was he met by such understanding and supportiveness, but he was accepted into the very heart of this great ministry, to serve the *Man of God*. Thus Fred came to carry the pastor's briefcase for him, make his milkless tea and caffeine-free coffee for him, run messages and errands for him and ride with him in the sporty Volvo that the church leased for him.

Being the senior pastor and leader of such a large and successful church, Walter Leakey was often asked to speak at other churches or conferences, either in Britain or overseas. As his assistant was not a female there were no reasons of propriety to pay for a second room when staying in hotels, so a double with separate beds would suffice. After speaking and 'ministering' for hours Walter would be aching in his muscles. He would shower, and with only a towel around him would ask his assistant if he wouldn't mind to help him apply a soothing cream to his neck and back, and lying himself face down on the bed, the assistant would oblige. Fred had already helped Walter with this once before, and now Walter came out of the bath, and he knew the question would probably come. As a former ballet-dancer Walter kept his body fit. He was nearing fifty but his body looked younger. Fred was only wearing the hotel bathrobe waiting to shower after Walter.

"Fred, would you be so kind as to rub the cream in for me? I could do with you kneading it in, if you don't mind. It helps if you're a bit rough," Walter said with a little glint in the eye.

"Of course, no prob," said Fred, jumping to his feet. Walter handed him the cream, laid the towel on the bed and his naked body on top.

"If you could do the soles of the feet up, don't stop until I say when, please".

Fred started on the feet and slowly worked his way up until he was inches from Walter's buttocks. Fred hoped he would soon say when, but at the same time hoping he wouldn't say.

"Thanks Fred, now if you would do the neck down please. This is wonderful after being on my feet for so long, you know. One mustn't neglect the care for the body in all this spirituality, Fred".

"No Walter, I quite agree". It was all he could think of saying, but thought immediately what a silly thing it was to say. The great Walter Leakey didn't need his agreement.

"No, no, no Fred, you need to put some more muscle into it."

Fred had carefully started to rub the cream in.

"Listen, why don't you sit astride me? That way you can use your weight. It's the only thing that really works."

Fred wondered if he should tell Walter that he wasn't wearing his boxers, but didn't want to seem reluctant to heed the master's word. He sat himself across Walter's back.

"Oh, sit a bit further down please", Walter ordered.

Fred wriggled down until his buttocks touched the pastor's. He couldn't help that his penis hardened a bit, but thought perhaps this was part of the lesson of self-control he had been promised. He tried to think of anything unromantic and unerotic. He thought of the Royal Family, his great aunt, a course in photography he planned to enrol in, how much he liked porridge in winter. Then Walter turned. Fred felt something touching his lower back that could only be one thing. Walter looked at him with the sweetest smile he had ever bestowed upon him, and Fred felt all resistance and guilt for his homosexuality vanish.

'So that is why he was so understanding,' he thought. Fred had only had a couple of fumbling sexual experiences. Walter was a seasoned and sensitive lover. He drew Fred near. The kisses and the touches thawed Fred's body, and permeated into his soul. He felt loved. Walter entered Fred, and they locked hands as the warmth of their bodies spread outwards into the extremities, and Fred knew he had never felt so happy, so complete, as in this lasting moment. As Walter put his arms around him and they lay tightly, Fred felt bare and unprotected, like a shell-less crab. But he was happy without the shell. He *wanted* to be utterly vulnerable in Walter's arms. They were his strength now, and his protection. The numbness of years of denial had evaporated and he felt as if his nerve-threads went from the centre of his soul right out to the pores of his skin, and there was absolute contact between his self and what he was and what he did. For the first time since puberty brought him in conflict with his faith, he felt truly good about himself.

Early next morning Frederic was awoken by the sound of sobbing supplications. He sat up in bed to see Walter prostrated on the floor crying, praying, begging.

"I can never undo what has been done, oh merciful God. I can but acknowledge my iniquity, my failure, my weakness, the depravity of this flesh. By the blood shed by Jesus I thank you, *thank you* (he was hoarsely crying this out as loud as hotel room walls permitted him) for cleansing this sin, for your forgiveness, for not allowing me to carry the just punishment for my sins, as it would crush me like an insect".

He laid sobbing face down for some minutes. The sobbing subsided, then silence. He finally got up, red in the face with bloodshot eyes, and stared in front of him. He had noticed Fred was awake and said to him in a flat tone of voice:

"I should also ask your forgiveness for taking you with me into sin. I have abstained from sexual activity for some time – as a form of fasting – and I can only admit that my animalistic needs got the better of my self-control. I am sorry I used you. I hope you will be able to forgive me".

"Of course…" Fred began, but Walter ignored him turning towards the bathroom.

I'm going to shower now, then go down to breakfast. I trust you will do what is right in the eyes of God and then come down and receive instructions for the day". He disappeared into the bath.

As Frederic heard the water being turned on he slid down on the floor and started crying soundlessly. He clambered unto his knees and tried to address the God that knows everything. But never had the heavens felt more closed, or the idea of our heavenly Father seemed more distant. God appeared to have shut the door and turned off the lights. Frederic nevertheless forced himself:

"Dear God, I know I have sinned against your will. Perhaps I tempted pastor Walter by my presence and what I did. Please, please forgive me. I am so terribly sorry." Tears flowed down his cheeks. "Please heal me, it is in your power to change me. To remove this demonic influence over my body. I reject it. I don't want it. Go Satan! Go! I want to serve the living God with all my heart, all my soul, all my… body".

The sobs took over at this point, the shaking and convulsions were so strong he could not speak; he only made cries of pain into his duvet to muffle the sound. After some time he noticed the hotel room door shutting, and he looked up. He was alone. He felt flat, worn, empty inside. He showered, dressed and went down. When he came to the breakfast room Walter was tucking into his bran cereals with fruit and decaf coffee, whilst next to him sat an apologetic looking twenty-something man, who had been honoured with the task of chauffeuring the Great Man of God. Fred walked over to the table and stood waiting insecurely for a second or two as Walter finished a point he was making to the chauffeur. He looked up at Fred.

"Well, get yourself some breakfast quickly. This young man has been waiting for a while already".

"No, no, p-p-p-p-problem" stammered the man.

He had awkwardly sat himself down next to Walter on the sofa-bench that ran along one of the walls, rather than opposite, on one of the chairs. Fred wanted rolls with egg and bacon, but he had the same as Walter, sat down on one of the chairs facing Walter and the other man, and felt embarrassed. Walter had regained a certain jollity, joking and asking questions about the chauffeur's interests and hobbies. Apparently he collected vintage comic books. Walter cracked witticisms and seemed excellently brilliant in the dull company. Fred looked at the vintage comic collector and thought, 'he is an honest man, unlike me'. He looked at Walter and knew he loved him. He expected to be sacked, but hoped he wouldn't. He would not resign. He hated himself for it, but knew that he now only lived for the next time Walter had a 'weakness'.

there was given to me a thorn in the flesh, the
messenger of Satan to buffet me, lest I should be
exalted above measure.
For this thing I besought the Lord thrice, that it might
depart from me.
And he said unto me, My grace is sufficient for thee: for my
strength is made perfect in weakness.

2 Corinthians XII; 7 – 9

Chapter X

In which our hero receives a visitor and realises something

The day came for Georg's arrival, and M went to Heathrow to meet him. Georg had never been chubby, but he'd always had a certain 'paddedness' so that even if, in his checked tweed jacket, brown cords and with his shuffling walk he seemed older than his years, he had maintained a healthy, almost ruddy look. His old look was part of what M loved about his friend. As a teenager M had felt it would fit him far better to be twenty-one. Not just to be able to order an alcoholic drink, but he felt twenty-one, he looked twenty-one, and was often mistaken for being twenty-one. His body had been too young for his soul. Now he was twenty-four, and people regularly thought him to be in his thirties when asked to guess; he liked that. Both Georg and M despised the 'cult of youth' that permeated modern popular culture. They didn't want to be eternally nineteen, nor part of the 'happening' scene, or on the 'cutting edge'. They admired the style of the eighty-year-olds, and heaped unforgiving scorn on the forty- or fifty-something's who tried to imitate the *yoof*; one of the most pathetic sins in their catalogue of human errors.

The two friends listened to music written either by dead or very nearly dead men, played by old men or recorded a very long time ago. When Georg had bought a flat a few years previous, the former owner had been an old lady who had decorated the flat very fashionably in 1978. Nothing had changed since: large floral patterned wallpapers, in varieties of green, brown and orange, lino flooring, and a practical, uncool kitchen in off-white and turquoise. Everybody thought Georg would start redecorating as soon as physically possible. M knew this would never happen. Firstly Georg would never waste energy on redecorating if everything was in working order. Secondly Georg would never spend time redecorating if he could rather spend the time listening to his music. Thirdly the style rather fitted with the furniture he already had: his '69-model mustard green sofa, his '65-model light brown coffee-table, the 1950s standing lamp and his 1970s book case. Georg still slept in the bed he had grown up with, complete with the feather down pillow of his childhood, which fitted nicely with the cloud-themed wallpaper of the bedroom. This was before anyone had thought up the term 'vintage' as a name for a fashionable style. Georg was simply old-fashioned or rather *non-fashioned*; too supreme to care, too aloof to give a damn, too elevated to feel compelled to change his style or redecorate a functional apartment to fit some contemporary taste. It was not so much a 'lifestyle choice' as a total indifference to making a choice at all. M, being more of an aesthete, recognised Georg's style as one, and smiled upon it. Despite his seemingly detached attitude to his own surroundings, Georg could recognise style and proportion, and the two would discuss taste theoretically, but he preferred the audial arts. Despite his conservative, not to say conservationist, appearance, Georg had no traditionalist limitations on his musical tastes. The Velvet Underground, Sex Pistols and other such luminaries of the alternative community had been early favourites. After becoming part of the Happy Life Church, M and Georg soon found they had a similar interest in music that lay beyond the trodden path of the anodyne, country-inspired Christian muzac so loved by modern churches. Through pale Scandinavian summer nights they forayed into the hidden treasures of old black-gospel recordings, as well as jazz and classical, assisted by endless helpings of Chinese tea. And when the tea-lights were going out, and the bright morning sun shone through the window the two friends looked at each other and thought 'a night well spent'. Some early mornings, just as the sun threatened to ascend, they would jump into Georg's green Ford and drive up to a hill-top where a small look-out tower stood, with stunning views over the sea, all the way to the very end of the earth. There they could share with countless previous generations, since the first dawn of man, the exhilarating birth of a brand new day, as the powerful, life-giving Helios spread out his luminous embrace over all creation. And all things that up to that point had been wrapped in the cold blue light of night were suddenly glowing with spots of golden radiance, dark shadows of contrast emphasising the shapes and forms of hills, trees, mountains, and the town's buildings. At such times M and Georg shared a primeval love of life itself.

It is of the Lord's mercies that we are not consumed,
because his compassions fail not.
They are new every morning:
great is thy faithfulness.
Lamentations III; 22 – 23

In the band Georg's contribution had been very tangible. His steady and musical drumming was the backbone of the group, and no little contributor to the moderate success they had enjoyed, travelling around the local area in Georg's green Ford, playing in all sorts of venues, from church functions to smoky pubs. It was therefore much sadder for Georg than he ever expressed that M left for London. Of course, M was doing it for God, to get his Christian service back on track, to devote his life to Jesus Christ, and so Georg had to be glad for it, to congratulate it and support it; all of which he did in genuine earnestness. In his quiet and unassuming way, Georg was in fact very devout, and when no trace of divided loyalty could be divined, it was because there was none. His fundamental loyalty was to God. When Georg had found faith at the age of twenty, he had been severely depressed after a failed romance and the early death of his father. He was not a man given to histrionics or excessive emoting. Nobody could tell he was depressed, as his outward demeanour did not really change very much. He just slowly retreated more into his own private world. The only one who noticed that something was not right was a childhood friend, who himself recently had been caught up in the revivalist frenzy going on at the Happy Life Church. He dragged Georg along, and in time Georg found the love of God to be steady and the revelation of eternal salvation a rock upon which to build a consistent and predictable existence. There was no changing with God, no development, no disappointment. It was what Georg needed and it satisfied him and made him happy. And thus he was the quiet, steady man, always to be relied upon. He would not suddenly change or fail to turn up on time. If he said he would do it, it would get done. In this he was a *man*.

And now M stood watching as Georg turned up at Heathrow. His heart sank when he saw the previously well-padded friend looking skinny in the now oversized tweed jacket, stooping as he shuffled along, pulling his suitcase on wheels. M knew that if he said nothing Georg would realise his shock at what had just a few months ago been a chunky fellow looking so shrivelled.

"Hullow, tiresome journey?"

"Not too bad, it's just that you have to walk for miles on end at this airport".

"Here, let me take the suitcase".

"Thanks".

Georg had tried to display his usual mixture of disdain and bemusement, but something was different. He seemed more tired, exhausted even. He walked even slower than usual, like the old man he looked like. M found it irritating; in the way he always found sick people an annoyance. His love for his friend made him forget his annoyance and look at him with a sense of sympathy and pity he knew Georg didn't want. Two years previous Georg had undergone heart surgery for some genetically caused defect on a heart valve. He had been extremely easily tired before the fault was discovered, but the operation had been a success and Georg recovered to old form fairly quickly. This sudden change of appearance was very untypical of him, and M feared it was cancer or some other dreadful affliction. M knew he had to cut to the chase. A direct question would dispel any embarrassment and make it OK for Georg to say as much as he wanted to.

"You've lost a bit of weight haven't you? Your jacket seems bigger on you".

"Yeah, it's these tablets I have to take since the operation, you know. They reduce my appetite. I tire a bit quicker too. But they've run all sorts of tests and all is fine, so…"

He shrugged his narrow shoulders and regained his bemused disdainfulness.

In the following days M would discover that this was no exaggeration. Having already grown accustomed to the high-speed pace of London life, forever rushing to and fro, just making it onto tubes and buses and arriving in a fluster, cursing traffic, M felt he now came to a crushing standstill. They seemed to be in everybody's way as they walked the crowded footpaths in slow motion. A momentary lapse saw M dash for an open tube door just as they were about to close. He held the doors as Georg heroically struggled aboard. M realised his mistake when he saw Georg's pale face, his empty stare as he stood grasping a bar and trying to recover from this sudden burst of physical exertion. When he recovered his ability to speak he asked if they could go and sit down at a café. They did and spent the next hour drinking coffee and talking, as Georg's natural colour slowly returned to his cheeks.

As planned they met up with pastor Sigmund, who entertained the two friends all the way to Christchurch with his latest theories of faith and church organising as well as *all* his views on current affairs. But even the absent minded and absorbed Sigmund perceived something was not quite right, when, after two hours of Sigmund's unique driving style, Georg wound down the window and vomited out of it. The total lack of shock and horror on Sigmund's face, which he had by effort managed to turn to a look of concern, made M want to laugh. He knew it would have made Georg laugh as well, but not now. Not now.

Georg had always been pedestrian in his tempo and temperament. His complete lack of sportiness was one of the qualities M liked about him, and shared with him somewhat. But what M had seen of his friend during these two weeks had unsettled him. After the Mission To Europe conference was over, and Georg had returned home, M was struck by a strange sense of loss. An uncharacteristic melancholy crept over him. The Georg he had once known was slowly ebbing away. Returning to the life he'd had before he left was clearly no longer on the menu.

Brethren, I count not myself to have apprehended: but this one thing I do, forgetting those things which are behind, and reaching forth unto those things which are before.
PHILIPPIANS III; 13

Chapter XI

In which our hero notices a change in Fred and a meeting takes place

It was a Monday morning, Walter and Fred returned to the church office from one of their ministry trips. M greeted Walter as he floated past reception, nose high, acknowledging M's greeting with the slightest flick of the head before disappearing into his suite of offices. Fred came a minute later laden with two pilot cases and a suit-bag, struggling through the doors. M held them open for him.

"Thanks."

"Good morning Fred, how was your weekend?"

"Yeah, good thanks. Very nice services and…"

He stared down in front of him a moment, then continued: "…I just have to check Walter's post." He went into the post-room, and came out empty handed.

"Oh, Monica must have taken it already. Well, he probably wants his stuff."

He hurried into Walter's office.

M thought his hurried behaviour out of character. 'He normally inquires with such sincere curiosity after my weekend. Probably exhausted after the trip,' thought M, and didn't know how right he was.

M and Fred had developed a rapport from the starting point of their shared 'Scandinavianness'. Danish and Norwegian are close languages; they could write messages in their respective native tongue, although for spoken communication English was easier on account of the peculiarities of Danish pronunciation. Fred had this particularly Danish quality that made M look forward to each time he ran into him in the corridor. It was an urban rurality, a conservative liberality, an old-fashioned modernity. All at the same time and without contradiction. Denmark was the most relaxed, laid back and continental of the three Scandinavian countries, a reason why so many from Norway – M's family included – holidayed in Denmark. Fred had large, blue eyes that looked at you with interest and toleration. They seemed to spark with interest just for you, and you felt accepted and at ease in his presence. You might even feel it is summer and you are on holiday in Denmark, and that you are eleven or twelve years old, and that you have met this boy who becomes your best friend, and you play through the eternal Scandinavian summer days, and you fall a little bit in love with him. When the holiday is over you promise to write to each other and you never do. And then next year you don't meet him again, and it leaves a sweet pain. But the memory of your friendship stays embedded in your memory, and reminds you with strange intensity of the summer when you stopped being entirely a child.

M hoped their friendship was not changing just because Fred had started working for the Senior Minister's office.

Tracey came out of her little office and stood straight in front of M, looking at him with her half-open Asian eyes and a very slight smile on her lips.

"Pete would like to see you M," she said, implying that M should start running, and she would take his place at the telephone.

M liked being called for a meeting. Especially when Tracey had to cover for him. He felt more important, more part of the daily business rather than somewhat on the side of it. He fluttered like a bird out of its cage down the corridor, past the long row of doors of small offices until he came to the big door that led into a big suite of offices: Pete Crowley's domain.

'It must be something important for Pete to call a meeting,' thought M. Suddenly it struck him: 'perhaps they know about Isaac'. An icicle burrowed his guts. 'No, no way. Let's just act normal'. He liked it when Pete's PA announced him. He entered Pete's office with the politeness of a schoolboy, and tried to look alert and friendly and relaxed.

"Sit down M. Tea?"

"Yes please"

"I've been watching you lately," said Pete, reading glasses perched on his nose. He continued moving papers from one pile to the next.

'Uh-oh, what now?' thought M.

"I know you're frustrated dividing your time between reception and caretaking work, and by gad I understand that working with that Finn is not the easiest thing in the world."

M gave a little nodding smile to signal he got the joke that wasn't quite a joke.

"But you have done it, and amazingly Ellina is crazy about your work. It's the only thing she *is* happy about at the moment." He stopped shuffling papers, and took the reading glasses off. "You've got on with the job, never complaining, never once have I seen you without that trademark smile of yours, never once have you whined, complained or lost your cheery disposition."

M felt increasingly pleased with himself, and thought that reading *How To Win Friends and Influence People* wasn't such a waste of time after all.

Pete looked at M with his frowning, big face.

"As you may be aware Dave has already left and Richard is leaving. Richard's already only part-time."

M had known for some time that these two church administrators were going, and the day Dave left was the only time M could remember seeing him look truly happy. Richard was cutting down his day-to-day involvement because his nerves could not take the strain anymore, although he would remain on the church board. Dave had been heartily fed up and had gone to work in his local satellite church. Moreover M knew Dave was the typical English whinger, Pete hated. Dave never really smiled, except in an ironic way when there was nothing really to smile about. The English were very good in a crisis, such as the Second World War, because of their lack of histrionics. They simply carried on carrying on. But when things were going well they were at a loss as to how to respond. Unlike in America, success is not uninhibitedly celebrated in Britain. Success is more a cause of embarrassment than joy, for a true Englishman, and it will never do to show on the surface that you revel in it. For Dave this came natural. Every little thing that went right he put down to unnatural and untypical luck, and everything that went wrong was grasped, as with relief, and talked about endlessly, as only to be expected. It exasperated Mr C. He was a man of forward action, constantly thinking of the next move, trampling through resistance making way on behalf of the preacher, pastor or business for which he was working. His attitude was closer to that of the American: get on with it, don't linger on your mistakes, get the next one right. Solution oriented, there is no such thing as a problem only *opportunidees!* But if this mentality did not come easily to a typical Englishman like Dave, it certainly didn't come any easier for the Finnish Ellina. Naturally morose as any Finn, her inbuilt negativity took the shape of a slow boiling anger, a seething geyser given to sudden outbursts at very low levels of provocation. And the levels of provocations at the Chelsea Chapel could sometimes be anything but low.

Over at the old church building in Chelsea, Francoise was the Inspector Clouseau of caretakers, doing the strangest things and explaining them in an accent far more outlandish than Peter Sellers' creation. Mr C had had quite enough of dealing with these characters directly since Dave left.

"The other thing that you *don't* know is that Tina is leaving (she was Paul's PA) and Tracey will take her place. Now, I can't take anymore of Ellina's lamenting every goddamn lightbulb to me, nor do I care to listen to Francois' explanations as to why he is feeding gypsies in the church car park with the senior minister's lunch. I want these people to report to *you*. Including the receptionists. All of 'em. You'll be my buffer. You will report to me directly. I have enough on my plate. I'm juggling ten balls in the air at the same time. I've seen the way you work, your attitude. You can cut the mustard and get the ducks in a row".

He leaned forward and sipped his tea. Then in a more buddy-like tone, as if M had stepped over the threshold to another level of intimacy:

"Listen, I don't wanna know the ins and outs of a duck's arse. Just give me the bottom-line".

He illustrated the bottom line by holding his palm out and making a sideway movement with his arm.

"Your title will be Assistant General Manager, and it will carry some clout. I will involve you when organising events as well, but we'll get back to that as and when. Now keep yourself in readiness. We'll meet with Walter later this week or early next when he will make you the formal offer. I just wanted you to know what was happening, and prepare you for it mentally. So just keep mum for the time being. Alright?"

"Yes, I…" M said, slightly stunned, but not entirely surprised. It was, after all, simply an acknowledgment of his talent and ability. It was as it should be. He had in a stroke gone from being the one who helped Ellina wash the loos to being Ellina's line manager, indeed all the caretakers' manager and the receptionists' manager – nearly a dozen people. The thought filled him with great satisfaction. Pete leaned back in his chair, put his arms behind his head and started shaking with quiet laughter.

"I do believe I've thrown you. Are you speechless M?"

M looked up from his reveries; "Oh sorry, I was just…"

"Listen, if you need more time to think about it…"

M cut him off: "Pete, I have absolutely no doubt in my mind that I want to work for you. Of all the people I have met here, of all the pastors and the staff, there is nobody I would rather work for."

M knew these words told Mr C that he'd rather work for him than Walter; Pete understood it and liked it.

"I mean, the thing is Pete, you remind me of my father in so many ways…"

An unusual softness came over Pete's face.

"Dear boy, I knew from the start that… you had something… you know… a quality, call it what you like, that you and I are going to get on…" He got up from his chair and walked around his enormous desk, grabbed M's hand and looked him deep in his eyes:

"Next week we'll meet with Walter to confirm your appointment, then I will gather all the caretakers and receptionists and tell them *you're* in charge. When you speak you will speak for *me*, with my authority. All right?"

"Yes Pete, thank you".

M felt strangely successful after the meeting. He had been truthful about whom he would rather work for, and also that Pete reminded him of his father. But he had also understood the value of saying the right thing at the right time, and he had achieved the sort of emotional response he wanted. Perhaps Pete had understood this and appreciated the skilfulness of it. M had no doubt that Mr C's trust in him was well placed.

PART II: Revelation

Seal not the sayings of the prophecy of this
book: for the time is at hand.

Revelation XXII; 10

CHAPTER XII

In which our hero has an interview with Walter,
goes to a staff meeting and makes a decision.

There were several things he had come to dislike about the previously affable Dane. Since Fred had been promoted right past M and into the Senior Minister's Office, he had become gradually more aloof, going around with a serious, frowny look on his face, as if he was genuinely important and carrying the worries of the entire church on his shoulders. He did not take the time to chat, he didn't joke in the same way anymore. Certainly not about Walter. M didn't like that sort of change in behaviour and countenance, especially when it was precipitated by a change in position. M could have understood it if Fred had been given real responsibility. But he was nothing more than a briefcase carrier, a tea-maker, a gofer. Who did he think he was anyway? There was an ambitious side to M, or was it a sense of entitlement? In any case, it pained him to see lesser men elevated above him. On the other hand he was genuine glad to be working with Pete. He knew it would afford him a greater chance of imprinting himself; he could create a little fiefdom, which would not have been possible had he been working directly under Walter.

As he and Pete entered Monica's office – the outer office to Walter's – M heard Walter admonishing Fred irritably. They followed Monica into Walter's spacious corner office. M had never been there before. It was L-shaped. Immediately on the left was a conference table, and in the far corner on the left, where the two lines of the L met, was a lounge-area with two large sofas separated by a low coffee table. A large walnut coloured desk with a modernistic black and chrome high back executive chair stood in the far right hand corner along with the tea and coffee making facilities and a small fridge. Monica went over to Walter and gave him some paperwork, they exchanged some muffled words, Monica went back out, and Walter turned to his guests.

"Hello Pete, M, how nice to see you," he smiled, then the smile disappeared a little too quickly. He gestured to the conference table, "tea, coffee?"

"A nice cuppa wouldn't go amiss," replied Pete. M thought it best to join in.

"Oh yes, tea please. Milk, two sugars!" The last remark he threw towards Fred. He felt pleased that Fred was fretting about making tea and coffee, whilst he, M, was having a proper meeting with the Senior Pastor. They sat down at the glass-topped conference table. The furniture seemed very futuristically modern in a late '80s sort of way. Dark, cherry coloured wood with dark glass. The sofas had large floral patterns. 'Probably chosen by his wife,' thought M.

"Fred, can you see to it, please," said Walter to Fred as he came over to the conference table with the paper-folder Monica had given him.

M felt pleased. "This is the proper order of things", he thought.

Walter put narrow, fashionable reading glasses on, and looked at the papers in the folder.

"Of course you know why you are here M…"

"Well, I *hope* I know why I am here," replied M.

Pete chuckled.

Walter looked up and smiled. He liked the reply but disliked it when others tried to be witty in his presence. He tried not to show it. Fred brought the tea, looking tired.

"Well Pete, have you not told the lad why he is here?" Walter looked at Pete over the rim of his glasses. Now Pete looked slightly irritated.

"Sure I have, he knows very well why he is here".

"So, you *do* know why you are here?"

M nodded and said, "yes, it seems I know why I'm here".

Walter smiled again. "Good, I am glad we all know why we are here". He glanced at Fred.

M liked feeling part of the joke. He felt he was more grown-up for it. Part of the big-boy's club.

Walter started mentioning how it had been reported that M had done very well at reception, as a caretaker, and when he had been given supervisory duties, he had executed them very well.

"Just remember M: this is not the army… although I sometimes wish it was," he looked at M and smiled an overbearing schoolmaster smile, then he looked at Pete who nodded and smiled knowingly.

He had in mind a couple of incidents when M had been the duty-supervisor over the Christmas period, when Tracey had been away. He had commandeered the caretakers and put pastoral calls through to the duty-pastors even if they didn't want to take them. One, an Indian fellow who liked to tell everybody that his name, Raj, meant something with "king", and that he was from the *north* of India (as if it made any difference to M) had been incandescent with rage as M had ignored his protestations and put through a particularly difficult parishioner. He had come storming down the corridor to put M in his place. M had given no ground, just told him to do his job as a pastor, in what might have been a slightly haughty voice. The Indian Raj had promised to complain to M's superiors. M had heard nothing, other than a couple of sarcastic asides from Pete about Indians generally. Now, Walter was making a subtle reference to it in such a way that M had the feeling he did not fully disapprove of what

M had done, but wanted him to mind the way in which he did it, so as not to be seen to be arrogant. 'Fine, I can do that,' thought M.

Walter went on to tell M about his new and improved salary, his title and the expectations as to presence at services. At least two on a Sunday, as well as *every* Wednesday evening and one Friday a month. There was a duty-rota for the Friday service.

M came away with slightly confused sentiments. He felt pride at having achieved such a responsible position in one of Europe's largest churches, and he wanted to do his best. On the other hand, he could not understand why they had to tell people which services to attend. Back in his old church he would simply go to every service possible. He had never seen it as a *duty* before.

One of the first practical changes for M was that he no longer had to sit in the reception every day answering calls, receiving visitors and sorting post. He was allowed to hire a new part-time receptionist to cover his shift. The new PM-receptionist was a lady of immense glamour and gloss. Of mixed African-Caribbean-Anglo descent, Barbara had the subtlety of dame Edna Everage, combined with the shallow bourgeoisie judgmentalism of Mrs Hyacinth Bucket. M enjoyed being the manager of people older than himself. In addition to Barbara M managed the morning receptionist Mary, a South-African Boer, Khoora, a young, stick-thin Algerian lady with large, curly hair and big puzzled eyes, Fido, the Bolivian gentleman with a thick Hispanic accent and neat dress sense. Tonji, a Ghanaian lady with a bubbly sense of humour, and of course, the hair-troll he had seen on his first visit, Agatha McGinty. Agatha was a volunteer. She was one of the Ugandan Indians who had fled Idi Amin's reign of terror in the 1970s. She never received money for her untiring efforts on behalf of the church. Seen as a saint for her unselfish service, M soon learned that being non-employed meant that she did not fit into any formal structure of accountability. She was a free agent, and M thought she probably preferred the perfectly selfish freedom of being outside the formal structure. He was, however, intent on including her as much as possible in all formal meetings for two reasons: no one knew as much as her about how things had been done in the church, and no one was present in church as often and as much as her. He wanted to know all there was to know from her, and he wanted her not to have the excuse of not having been informed.

Then there were the caretakers at the old church building: Francoise, half French, half Algerian, and John Deroome, English. John had made clear his demand that he would only work the daytime shifts Mondays to Fridays, and only at the church building. Francoise had been covering all other shifts: all evenings as well as every weekend from early morning to late. Agatha would order him around in a way she never could with John, and Francoise was only too willing to step to it. He was extremely agile: thin, with sinewy muscles, and sprang from place to place with boundless energy. But M realised very quickly that what was going on with Francoise was quite illegal. He was working far more than what was allowed, and more importantly for M: far more than what was reasonable to expect. He would sooner or later burn out, quit and leave a huge gap to fill. It was urgent to sort it out.

M was now expected to attend the weekly staff meetings on Wednesday afternoons. He had been envious as he had seen his colleagues gather for their weekly pep-talk by pastor Walter, and not being able to join them, having to stay on reception and man the phones.

The purpose of the staff meeting seemed to be to keep the large body of staff somewhat on the same course. As with the other church services, this gathering also started with a hymn. The worship leader brought his electrical keyboard, and laughingly took the staff with him into a buoyant modern hymn with lots of hand-clapping and strange syntax to make the awkward words fit the modern style melody and rhythm. M had a deep dislike of modern hymns. They sounded like bad pop-music, the words were often inane, the theological substance questionable, and the implicit expectation of a happy-clappy participation irritatingly close to the songs of children's entertainers. M also disliked the formulaic way a bouncy upbeat song was always followed up by a song that was slow and syrupy to encourage more intense emotional engagement. M thought it only encouraged self-conscious, introspective emoting.

During the slow song Walter would enter the room quietly – sometimes he seemed to just materialise at the front – where he would stand looking disapprovingly on the staff. On this day he stood with eyes closed. When the song had finished there were murmurs of prayers, some quiet babbling in tongues, some louder. At length Walter looked up with glassy, tired looking eyes. The murmuring died down. There issued from Walter a sense of guilt and inadequateness that permeated the staff meeting, making it not so much an oasis of encouragement and recharging of spiritual batteries, as a desert of endurance, deflating any remaining energy one might have brought into the meeting. A particular strand that had been running through the staff meetings lately was prayer and Bible reading. A small movement of the hand indicated that the employees might sit. Then Walter stood in silence. Just as it was getting uncomfortable, with people wondering if something might be seriously wrong, he spoke. His eyes were fixed at some distant point above the staff members' heads.

"A little while ago a staff member complained to me of feeling tired and exhausted," he said quietly, as if relaying a confession of depraved debauchery. "This person, he or she, said it was difficult to keep the energy up to do all the things that needed doing, and have time on one's own with the Lord. This person no longer works here. He or she felt '*burnt out*'." – Long pause – "Burnt out in the service of the Lord. It is not the first time, and it won't be the last. And why? Why would a person in the Lord's ministry burn out? Too many meetings? Perhaps. Too much to do? Possibly. Too many people to care for, too many projects and conferences and demands? The needs are great and seemingly endless. Yes, I admit, I ask a lot of my co-workers. But I can assure you, I ask nothing of you that I ask not of myself, and I punish myself a lot more than I would ever allow for any of you!"

The last bit was said with the deep snarling of a wounded animal. "THEN WHY DON'T I BURN OUT?" he shouted. People jumped in their seats. "Burn-out is a way for the devil to steal you away from your ministry, and the ministry away from you. How many of God's servants have been torn away from the path and plan God had for them by burn-out? Many more than I care think about. But who doesn't burn out? And why? Let me tell you what really causes burn-out: *too little* time spent in prayer!"

M could sense the feeling of discomfort spreading like a mist over the congregated staff, as faces were screwed into earnest-worried grimaces; all trying at once to portray an understanding of the gravity with an undertone of, 'but of course *I* already pray for hours on end', betrayed by a streak of guilt, suppressing too hard the urge to look around at the other faces.

"Too little time spent *alone* with the Lord", continued Walter. "It is during this time of earnestly seeking God that you are replenished and re-energised".

M could not grasp this cliché of 'seeking God'. Surely he had already found God; or rather God had found *him*. Moreover, He had given M his Holy Ghost and all the Abrahamic blessings were supposed to belong to all believers in Christ by *faith*. What was it he was supposed to *seek*?

And if ye be Christ's, then are ye Abraham's seed, and heirs according to the promise.

GALATIANS IV; 28 – 29

On the other hand, M had come to this church after what he believed to be a calling from God. Perhaps He wanted M to see things from a different angle, discover things hitherto hidden or veiled. M decided to go along, to be open, humble and receptive.

Walter continued: "when and how you pray I cannot go into. I have written about it in my book *The Spiritual Sword*. But I have been shocked to find out that many staff members do not read through the Bible at least once every year. Time is not an excuse. I am extremely busy, but I use a reading schedule that enables me to read through the Bible four times every year. I know you all hear the Word quoted in services, and you read snippets here and there, but there is something special about getting the entire kaleidoscopic view of the Word of God. It gives you a better sense of the continuity of revelation."

'What rubbish' thought one part of M. 'Doesn't he know how the Bible was put together? By men deciding to put certain things in, take certain things out and edit the order to serve a decided upon narrative'. 'Oh but', said the other part of M, 'the Bible is a result of a miraculous intervention by the Spirit of God working through men to produce a unique physical manifestation of the Word of God as spoken to mankind for our need in the present world'. M decided to go with the latter voice.

"So, I have instructed Monica in my office to draw up various versions of this plan. Minimum is twice through the Bible in a year, up to six times a year. The beauty of this system is that it takes you through the New Testament twice for every once you go through the Old Testament. So when you have read the Old Testament twice, you will have read the New Testament four times." Walter declared.

M thought it peculiar how Walter lit up when he spoke of these technicalities. He seemed to get the eagerness of a schoolboy, so beaten into submission that only the thought of pleasing his elders can give him any sense of joy, or reprieve from the oppressive, ever present, guilt.

After the staff meeting M decided, along with most staff members, to start on the reading plan. He also took to heart Walter's admonition to spend time on one's own in prayer to get closer to the Lord, and avoid burnout. It was logical. If man can be likened unto the new Smart car, prayer is the process of connecting the power cord to the mains (God) and receiving a charge-up. The more time spent in prayer and Bible reading the more spiritual electricity would stream into the batteries of one's inner man.

But ye, beloved, building up yourselves on your most holy faith,
praying in the Holy Ghost
JUDE I; 20

Thus the alarm-clock was set for 5:15 am, and by 5:30 am, cup of strong tea in one hand, Bible in the other, M was on his knees using one of the Psalms as a basis for a prayer. An hour later he rose, readied himself and set off for work at the church, feeling very pleased with himself. On the train he took out his Bible and the reading plan and started on The First Book of Moses, Genesis, chapter I: "*In the beginning God created the heaven and the earth. And the earth was without form, and void; and darkness was upon the face of the deep. And the Spirit of God moved upon the face of the waters.*"

M had a feeling of starting all over again. He recalled the greedy hunger with which he had devoured the good book when he had first become a believer at fourteen. Now, as a more mature believer the enthusiasm of youth had to be replaced by the discipline of adult spirituality. God had brought him here for a reason. Perhaps this was the start of a breakthrough, the natural next step away from the complacency of habit to the discovery of new, great things.

When I was a child, I spake as a child, I understood as a child, I thought as a child: but when I became a man, I put away childish things.

1 Corinthians XIIII; 11

Some staff members had noisily declared how they had started on the four times a year plan. No doubt they would fall off quietly after a while. M had gone for the sensible twice a year (which meant the Old Testament twice, the New Testament four times) because he knew he could go through with it. What with travelling, work, services and studies, M found that he had not been mistaken in thinking there would be limited time for additional reading. He arose at a quarter past five for his hour of prayer, then he read on the bus, on the train, in his lunch hour, and on his train home. Going home in the evening (when he did not have services to attend) he found himself tired and falling asleep. He reasoned that the New Testament is in a way more important to a Christian, so he decided to read only the New Testament text in the morning and in the lunch hour, and then Old Testament going home. He had just reached the genealogy bit of the books of Moses and it was like wading through quicksand wearing led-boots.

Suddenly opening his eyes, he found he had been asleep and gone three stations past his own and had to dash out of the train just as the doors were closing. He went across to the other platform. It was another five minutes until the train going the other way would arrive. He took his Bible out of his bag and continued reading. But his mind wandered off, he had no concentration. He gave up and stared into nothing. The train arrived. He boarded. It was nearly empty. M sat down. Behind the seat, on the sill, someone had discarded a copy of *The Times*. M picked it up absentmindedly to pass time by flicking through. He opened it on the opinion and editorial pages. A surge of energy fuelled his concentration, and he devoured an article on tax-policy in the six minutes it took to go back to the right station. He took the paper with him, and as he had his beans on toast supper, he hoovered up all the commentaries and letters to the editor. Afterwards he felt glad he had found it, as well as a certain mild elatedness in having been brought up to date with all the latest current issues. Then his eyes fell on his dog-eared Bible, lying there all by itself like an abandoned teddy bear, and he felt a sting of guilt. He then resolved that as the Word of God is so important, he should only read it in the morning when his concentration was on top. That way he could pick up a newspaper to read on his way home with his *tired* mind.

The next day he followed the plan. He bought *The Times* in the morning, and packed it into his bag. All day he looked forward to the journey home when he would unfold the large broadsheet and smell it. He loved the huge size of it, the style of writing, the logo, the history, the whole feel of it. He would read the editorials and commentaries first. Then letters to the editor. He loved the way they always started with "Sir…" Then flick through the news, pause at political news, then everything else.

The next morning, as he stopped to pick up his *Times* he stole a few glances at the headlines before putting it into his bag. He got a seat on the train and took out his Bible. He was falling a little behind on the reading plan, but he felt sure he could catch up at the weekend. He started on the Apostle Paul's Letter to the Romans, and having read through the felicitations was feeling droopy. His eyelids felt as if weights were attached to them and they shut. He awoke with a start at the next station. He stared at the open page before him; the letters didn't seem to want to cooperate. It was like trying to eat cold, stale porridge. He thought longingly of the newspaper in the bag, but carried on ploughing through the Letter to the Romans.

He prayed: "Satan, get behind me in Jesus' name. Man shall not live by newspapers alone, but by every word that proceedeth out of the mouth of

God. Holy Spirit, shed your life-giving light on these words, make them come alive. Jesus *is* the Word, He is the bread of heaven, I command my spirit in Jesus' name to open up to the revelation knowledge that will issue forth from these printed letters".

This commanding prayer seemed to help. The words came more alive. He read on: "*For therein is the righteousness of God revealed from faith to faith: as it is written, The just shall live by faith.*" The just shall live *by faith*. His eyes stayed at this sentence. "*The just shall live by faith*". It was the very cornerstone of Protestantism. The sentence that had kick-started Martin Luther's rebellion against the popeism of old. The basis for the entire faith-movement in which M's own beliefs had been fashioned. The just shall live *by faith*. What was he trying to do with this duty reading? It was killing the joy of reading the Word of God. It was reducing the quality of revelation into a mechanical act of passing one's glance over printed letters on a piece of paper. It was against everything that was in his spirit and soul. M put the Bible into his bag and took *The Times* out. Released from a guilty conscience he read the paper.

That evening he had bought himself a nice piece of scrumptious chocolate cake. He made a pot of coffee and set down with the cake, coffee and Bible and enjoyed reading the rest of the letter to the Romans. At some point in the letters to the Corinthians he had fallen asleep on the sofa. At 3 am he awoke with a very stiff neck. The Bible had slid down on the floor, he felt cold and rose slowly, groaning as he stumbled to the bathroom. He undressed and crept under the duvet.

He was awoken by the sun shining on his face. He felt better than he had done in a long time. It was 8 am, he had overslept. No time for an hour of prayer. He sang a hymn as he showered, shaved and dressed, then hurried to the bus stop. At the train station he saw the paper stand at the newsagent as a welcoming committee; all the nice pristine newspapers lined up waiting for him. As the reading schedule had been upset anyway, he reasoned he would catch up during the weekend. He sat down on the train with *The Times* and felt a little happiness. He was a well-dressed gentleman reading *The Times*. It was a role he liked.

Chapter XIII

In which our hero has a conversation with Pete, hears some bad news
from the hometown and meets someone unexpectedly

M liked to arrive early at the office. He would be there by 8am every day, and not leave until 6 or 7pm. He had read in a management book that a good senior executive should be able to get everything done in five ten-hour days. And as he also followed the advice in E.W. Kenyon's *Signposts on the Road to Success* that, 'one should always work, not to the salary one has, but to the salary one wants to have'. M thought that a fifty-hour week, plus the church services, was not excessive. M discovered that Pete also liked to arrive early. A habit of an early morning coffee meeting developed. It was at one such coffee conference that M remembered he hadn't seen Fred for a while. What with his own busyness of getting into the swing of things, and Walter going on a speaking tour taking Fred with him, the Dane had fallen off M's radar lately. Now Walter had been back a few days but not Fred.

"Is Fred on holiday or something, Pete?" M asked innocently as Mr C perused a long list of tasks M had compiled on a yellow legal pad. He stopped reading and looked at M over the rim of his reading-glasses.

"Oh, I see. You don't have access to much gossip then, do you?"

M took that as a compliment.

"I don't Pete. Haven't heard anything. What's going on?"

Pete leaned back in his creaking chair. He took a bite of a croissant and a sip of coffee. It was clear to M that Pete wanted to tell him something, but was chewing over whether it was right to tell it or not so he tried not to look to curious or interested. 'Whatever it is, it is not really my concern,' he thought still feeling curious, wanting to be 'in the know'.

"Well…" said Pete slowly. "… I can't really give you any details… but Fred has threatened to take Walter to a tribunal because he… [sip of coffee]… believes himself… [bite of a croissant]… what should I say, wrongly treated at work. So there's a bit of a hoo-hah at the moment".

Quite a few thoughts went through M's mind at that moment, some of them close to the truth. But as he didn't know, and found it unsuitable to probe. M simply nodded and sighed, "Well, Walter does run them hard".

At this Pete spluttered his coffee, "Ha! Yes, very *hard* indeed, ha ha!"

And with this nudge-nudge, wink-wink they left the matter in the mutual misunderstanding drawer and moved on to more pressing matters.

*For this cause God gave them up unto vile affections: for even
their women did change the natural use into that which is
against nature:
and likewise also the men, leaving the natural use of the woman,
burned in their lust one toward another;
men with men
working that which is unseemly, and receiving in themselves that
recompense of their error which was meet.*

ROMANS II; 26, 27

Being Danish Fred loved his beer, and no less for having grown up in a church. It had been increasingly a comfort he sought, as the periods of coldness from Walter grew longer and the passion ever more heated and violent. He had wanted to spank Fred, and at first Fred thought this a fun, kinky sort of idea. But the beatings became increasingly severe and left painful marks. When Fred intimated he didn't care for it anymore Walter grew quietly furious and the periods of frost prolonged. Walter could be such a sensitive lover. His touches opened up a range of sensations of physical pleasure for Fred that had deeper spiritual resonance than many of the acts they went through with in church to signify worship. In the act they melted together in a way that went beyond the mere physicality of the act; their souls truly merged and no words were ever needed.

The tenderness gave way increasingly to a sadistic streak in Walter. The coldness of the frosty periods had crept in to the sexual encounters. Fred was treated harshly in the office and with little warmth in the lovemaking. Walter seemed to be a robot demanding to download himself on Fred once in a while. Perhaps he thought it was less sinful if neither of them enjoyed the relationship. Fred didn't really care anymore. Who was this cruel, horrible God he purported to believe in anyway? Why had He made, or allowed both him and Walter to become as they were, and then condemn it in His word? Some argued it was not God as such but the sinful nature of man, as corrupted by the original sin, that enabled this demonic influence to take hold. Fred had his entire life accepted this narrative, always hoping against hope in what the Bible teaches; that Christ's redemptive work, his dying on the cross, taking our iniquities, sins and deceases upon himself had brought healing and liberation from original sin to those who believe in Him.

Surely he hath borne our griefs, and carried our sorrows: yet we
did esteem him stricken, smitten of God, and afflicted.

But he was wounded for our transgressions, he was bruised for our
iniquities: the chastisement of our peace was upon him; and with
his stripes we are healed.
Isaiah LIII; 4 – 5

But Fred had believed in Him all his life, so had his parents. And yet... yet
he was never healed from this abnormality. And now he had seen first hand
that even Walter, this Great Man of God, this highly successful preacher, pastor
and example to thousands, was not healed either. Either God was cruel or He
was powerless. Or else He simply did not exist. It was all a giant fairy-tale, and
he was suffering now because he believed in it. Fred had always found boys
attractive. But the relationship with Walter was the first time he had felt anything
more than mere physical attraction or romantic friendship. This was, Fred had
to suppose, love, and it was bloody horrible. He had carried on longer than he
had wanted to out of loyalty to Walter, or to God, or to the church. He wasn't
sure. Then one day he exploded. He declared to Walter he would report him to
the authorities for the hours he had been pressurized to work, the mental and
emotional strain he had been put under, for the abuse of power and trust to get
sex. All the hurt and humiliation stopped confusing him and instead he felt cold
and clear and in control. He reeled off the charge list like a prosecutor, whilst a
dumbstruck Walter collapsed into a chair and started trembling, tears in eyes.

"Fred, we can talk about this. Don't do anything rash! Think of the
thousands of people who look up to me Fred".

"Why they look up to *you* I don't know anymore!"

"Neither do I Fred. It is the grace of God, purely the grace of God."

"Grace? No, it's hypocrisy and deception, a swindle, that's what. And it has to stop!"

"Fred, Fred, Fred, *please* listen.

"I am not listening to you anymore. You disgust me".

"Okay, okay, yes I understand that. I disgust myself too. But, please, can you talk to Pete? You like Pete don't you? Can Pete please have a chat with you before you make up your mind as to what to do?"

Fred was never able to be angry for long. Although he felt a burning hatred for the cowering pulp of a human being in front of him, there was also something vulnerable, pitiful, about him that Fred couldn't help feeling sorry for.

"Why, what is there to talk about?" he said defiantly.

"He can… he is able to be more objective. Just talk it through. Please be reasonable. You can still do whatever you resolve… after you have spoken to him".

Fred stood motionless for a little while. He had already made up his mind, but he wanted Walter to suffer the wait. At length he replied.

"Alright. I will talk to Pete."

"I am so sorry Fred. So terribly sorry, I have been an awful fool".

"Oh shut up!"

Fred left.

Pete had his own way with young men. He did perhaps not understand homosexuality, but he did understand homo*sociality*. He had the natural chumminess; the palness and matiness that made him connect with young guys in the unforced, relaxed and friendly way that Walter could never achieve. The talk was supposed to take place in the office, but Pete understanding this would leave Fred in the wrong frame of mind, suggested otherwise:

"Fred, old bean. Why don't we get outta here, this place gets to me sometimes".

This effectively connected with Fred's feelings.

"Let's have lunch at a nice pub I know. Just a small, local that serves some decent grub. They also do a nice bitter. You don't mind a bitter do you?"

They sat down in a brown corner. Pete asked if Fred had tried shepherd's pie. He hadn't. Pete went to order and came back with a couple of Carlsbergs.

"Look, they had Carlsberg. Let's drink to your country, eh?"

They finished the beer, then Pete fetched them a pint each of the house cask ale to go with the pie. At the end of the ales Fred was prepared to be talked into giving the fight up.

"Fred", Pete said in a confessional tone of voice, "these *Great Men of God*" (he indicated the inverted commas with his fingers) sometimes have great weaknesses. For some it is sex, for others it is money, or alcohol, pills, you name it. They're not perfect. They're not saints. They are broken vessels, but the important thing is that they are *empty* vessels. Willing to let God fill 'em, and use 'em to touch thousands of people. That is why I, having seen so many of them up close, seen what others don't see, still carry on working for them. I know for every one who is hurt or offended ten, a hundred or even a thousand is helped. So then the question becomes: is my hurt so bad that it is worth ruining a ministry that helps so many? If we weigh it up on the scales (he held his hands up like the two cups on the scales of Justice) *me* on one side, thousands of parishioners being helped on the other…"

He allowed the conclusion to be unspoken. Fred got the message. Who was he to destroy a ministry? Was he simply being selfish? He rubbed his eyes as he tried to think. He was feeling drowsy and confused.

"I suppose you're right Pete, but… I don't want anyone to… to go through the same, you know."

Pete put a fatherly hand on Fred's shoulder.

"That is precisely what I expected you to say. We think in the same way, you and I. I can assure you that we will put procedures in place. I'll make sure of it. This will not happen again. Listen!"

He straightened up and slapped Fred lightly on the thigh, as if he had just had a bright new idea.

"Tell you what, I will get them to give you six months salary. It will give you some time to think. Whether you want to stay and find another job or go back to Denmark, it will be your own choice. At the same time I will implement internal procedures to ensure that Walter does not travel alone with young men again. Don't you think that's for the best?"

By now Fred *wanted* to say "yes".

"I don't know Pete, it's…"

"Listen… (Pete lowered his voice conspiratorially) a legal fight will cost you money, it will take time, it will sap all your energy. You have to stand up in public and spill the beans on everything you and Walter have done together. At the end of it they may just find you a 'spurned lover' and decide you went along willingly, thus award you nothing. The cost may be phenomenal, and the only thing you'll be sure to have achieved is the destruction of Walter's ministry, his family and the lives of all the people who trust him and look up to him and who have their work in the ministry. There are families with mortgages depending on the income from the church. Is it worth risking all that for…?"

He looked deep in to Fred's eyes. Fred averted his eyes, and heaved a sigh. Of course his decrepit, sinful little self was not worth it. How could he have been kidding himself. A worthless worm like him, against all those worthy, honest, earnest, if deceived, servants of God.

*Ye have heard that it hath been said, An eye for an eye, and a
tooth for a tooth:
but I say unto you, That ye resist not evil: but whosoever shall
smite thee on thy right cheek, turn to him the other also.*
MATTHEW V; 38-39

"I suppose not".

Pete produced an envelope with two papers inside.

"Fred, mate, listen, let us agree that I will look out very carefully in future, make sure we put the procedures in place. You will know that by dealing with the matter in this way you have achieved the protection of other young men – which is what you wanted, right?"

Fred nodded. "And you get to walk away with a small – actually not that small – token, a financial apology, which is at least enough for you to get some time to think and… go your own way. Are we agreed, my friend?" Pete offered his hand.

Fred looked at the hand for a fraction of a second, and in that instant he knew he couldn't refuse it. Knew that it would be too dogmatic and self indulgent to throw aside all the points Pete had made and stubbornly go on with his revenge. After all, he *had* gone along willingly. He had stayed. And as a Christian he was suppose to turn the other… cheek. He'd get the money. His parents wouldn't have to know, which was perhaps more important than anything to him. And it would be terribly rude to refuse to shake an outstretched hand. He grabbed Pete's hand and they shook.

"Good man" said Pete, and laid the papers in front of Fred. "Now, for the formalities. We'll just have to have these signed for the records. Fred signed them without reading through. A single teardrop fell on his signature.

Put on therefore, as the elect of God, holy and beloved, bowels of
mercies, kindness, humbleness of mind, meekness, long-suffering;
forbearing one another, and forgiving one another,
if any man have a quarrel against any:
even as Christ forgave you,
so also do ye.
COLOSSIANS III; 12 – 13

For a few weeks M had been emerged in preparations for the church's big Easter Conference at the Royal Albert Hall. There were countless memos to write, purchase orders to push through the accounts department, lists of things to buy, order, do, plan, sort. Names to list for jobs and roles, most of whom were unpaid volunteers. Each and every person had to have a badge, colour-coded according to level of access. M was pleased to be the only one Pete decided would have a badge with the same title as himself: 'Event Manager'. In the last couple of weeks M spent all his waking hours at work. He didn't mind. He had come to the Chelsea Chapel to serve God; to help in any way he could to expand the Kingdom of God. This church, with its vision of a Metropolitan Church Network – 2,000 satellite churches by the year 2000 – inspired evangelical Christians around the world. M had put aside his childish desire to be a filmmaker or musician or writer, or any of those creative occupations that had taken so much time back in the hometown. Now he was doing a job that would advance the Word of God in a world that desperately needed to be saved. Although disappointed at never becoming comfortable with Walter Leakey, he had to acknowledge that his leadership was highly successful. So if staying back in the office until 9 pm was the price to pay to be part of it, M was more than willing to pay it.

The last planning meeting had arrived. Pete asked if everything was packed and ready to go to the Royal Albert Hall in the morning. Diego Hezpionsa, the irritable Spanish head of audio confirmed impatiently. The messy but competent Ben Carton confirmed – with a disclaimer for anything unforeseen that he had not foreseen. The perpetually exasperated Madonna of the Christian book-trade, Sara Grühn (who, like M had also decided not to do the second year of the Bible College) confirmed in an efficient German way. M also confirmed, in a cold Norwegian way that seemed to take offence at even being asked such a question. Pete presided over the meeting as the King of the

Mountain Hall. Big and compact and fired up by the chaotic energy of event planning, with his large head containing a capacious brain that remembered everything, looking forward to a week of continual crisis management. It was what he loved best.

"Right everyone! Better get a few hours beauty sleep. *You* need it Ben, HA-HA-HA! And then I will see you all here tomorrow at sparrow's fart, bright eyed and bushy tailed!". His belly danced up and down like a bathing ball, at this last witty comment. M smiled and stored the expression for future use.

The conference got off to a good enough start. Everyone was buzzing about and the operations team could enjoy the relative calm during services to sit in the back rooms and drink endless cups of bad coffee and strong tea. Ben got on with what he was master of: controlling and directing the cameras filming the services. Diego reigned supreme behind his enormous sound desk and Sara fretted about ensuring the book displays were perfectly balanced and proportioned, getting apoplectic fits over every little detail even slightly out of order. M was beginning to feel unwell. The strain and stress of recent weeks had worn him down, and now, whilst sitting down in the back room, influenza symptoms washed over him. Pete noticed M's paleness.

"You all right, my friend?" he asked.

"Actually, no, not really. I feel horrible. Headache, sore throat… I'm coming down with something for sure. What a bloody nuisance". M closed his eyes.

"Well listen" Pete started comfortingly, "everything here is tickety-boo. You've done a great job organizing all the operational stuff. Seriously I have never been so relaxed at a conference before. We can manage a couple of days without you. Go home and rest, and get back for the last day when we need you again for the packing up".

M felt better for the praise. And he was grateful to be able to go home and sleep. But when he went out to the car park to drive home, he found that Charlie Hatkinson had parked his car blocking M's car. M went back in, and to the rooms reserved for the Senior Pastor and his entourage. He found Charlie waiting to be let in to see Walter.

"Oh, Charlie, I need to go, I'm not feeling very well. You're car is blocking mine. Could you move it, or could I borrow the keys please?".

Normally the caretakers would take the various pastors' and visitors' car keys and shuffle the cars about as needed. But after he received as a gift from a church member a gleaming hunting green Jaguar, Charlie never handed over his keys. Being at the Royal Albert Hall, M thought, Charlie would probably not mind, as it was simply a matter of backing it up, then putting it back. Lots of space. Charlie, who only recently had been promoted to Second Pastor, was looking serious and full of the sense of his own importance. Without meeting M's eyes, he waved him off saying, "Not now, later!" then disappeared into Walter's lair. M fumed. He turned on his heel and marched out, where he met Pete.

"What's the matter now?" asked Pete, who noticed the look on M's face.

"Charlie Hatkinson, what a little prick!"

Pete burst out laughing.

"Why? What happened?"

Pete looked grave as M relayed Charlie's arrogant haughtiness.

It didn't take too long before another car moved and M could get out. He drove away. As he was about to cross Kensington High Street he noticed an Anglican church he had seen several times before. Now he wanted to see the inside of it. He hadn't been in a main stream 'state-church' since he went with his family as per the Christmas tradition, many years ago. He entered the empty church. Despite the warming sunshine outside, it was dark and cool inside. And quiet. He sat down on a wooden bench and looked up at the altar. A peacefulness he hadn't felt for weeks, even months, slowly descended unto him. He rested his folded hands on the pew in front, then bowed his head and rested it on his folded hands.

"Dear God" he prayed. "I think I have been… blind. I ask you now, I beg you, to show me the way forward".

At that moment he heard the birds chirruping in the trees outside the stained glass windows. Perhaps they had been twittering all the time and that he only noticed it at that moment. He felt a contentedness he'd never had time to feel at Chelsea Chapel. It was clear for M that God had answered him, and that he now had to work out what the answer meant for him.

And, behold, the Lord passed by, and a great and strong wind rent the mountains,
and brake in pieces the rocks before the Lord; but the Lord was not in the wind:
and after the wind an earthquake; but the Lord was not in the earthquake:
and after the earthquake a fire; but the Lord was
not in the fire: and after the fire
a still small voice.

1 KINGS 19; 11 – 12

The experience in the Anglican church left M with a strange feeling in the days and weeks afterwards. A bit like when one has had something very peculiar to eat, and the memory of the flavour stays with you afterwards, until you feel you simply must try it again. M had started to feel like a visitor at the Chelsea Chapel. He had been a sojourner – now he was an outsider. 'If people in this church keep having burn-out', he thought, 'if leaders behave in the way I have seen… where is the power of the Holy Spirit?' If leaders and Christians in one of the greatest, most influential charismatic churches in Europe, are no better than anyone else, then where *is* the difference that the baptism in spirit and fire was suppose to make to one's life? Perhaps all those terribly important theological differences that was supposed to set the charismatic Pentecostalists apart had no real bearing on the way the individual Christian lived his life. And if so, then the whole construction he had built his Christian experience on, the idea of not being religious in the traditional sense, but rather a true follower of Jesus Christ – driven by the power endowed on the day of Pentecost – was nought.

Then some news came:

News one:

M was awoken by the telephone ringing one Saturday morning.

"Hello?"

M's old friend Tom, from the home church in Norway was on the other end of the line.

"Good morning. How are you M?"

"Yah, all right thanks". Tom had never telephoned M since he'd moved to London.

"Afraid I have some bad news. It's Georg."

"Oh, what about him?"

"He's become rather ill. Something to do with his kidneys not working properly. He needs to undergo dialysis every other day."

"Is it possible to talk to him?"

"He's finding it a bit difficult to speak… although you could probably talk *to* him"

M took down the number and called the hospital. Georg was sleeping or resting and couldn't be disturbed.

The phone rang again. It was M's father.

"You heard about Georg?"

"Yes, Tom just called. I tried the hospital, but he was resting."

"I meant to call you some time back. Met Georg in town a little while ago. I was driving the people carrier and offered him a lift. He seemed very grateful. But you should've seen how he struggled to get in. Like a 90-year-old. I felt terribly sorry for him. And now he's on dialysis. Your mom and I will pop around and see him as soon as we can."

Is any sick among you? let him call for the elders of the church; and
let them pray over him, anointing him with oil
in the name of the Lord:
and the prayer of faith shall save the sick, and the Lord shall
raise him up;
and if he have committed sins,
they shall be forgiven him.
Confess your faults one to another, and pray one for another, that
ye may be healed.
The effectual fervent prayer of a righteous man
availeth much.
JAMES V; 14 – 16

News two:
After this conversation M felt the need to walk around on his own and think. He went down to central London. There is no place like a big city for being on your own. M liked to wander about in the side streets, away from the throngs of tourists, and somehow he ended up in Soho. He walked down the seedy streets feeling slightly embarrassed. A vulgar looking woman invited him to come and enjoy a peep show. He looked away blushing, and the lady laughed a hoarse, coarse laughter. M hurried along and popped into the nearest coffee shop. He went straight to the counter and ordered a cappuccino with an extra

shot. As he waited he looked around. There weren't many seats on the ground level, so he decided to go downstairs. As he descended he saw a number of two-seater sofas with a high backs, forming almost a sort of protective shell. It reminded M of the old bubble shaped public phone booths that used to be in airports and corridors of public buildings. Only these 'booths' were made of upholstered fabric, and each held a pair of guys of the same gender occupied in snogging and cuddling. M quickly realised he had wandered into the wrong sort of place and was going to ask to have his coffee transferred to a paper cup. But as he ascended the stairs and neared the counter, a familiar face was standing there ordering. M felt a mixture of embarrassment over meeting someone he knew in a place like this, and curiosity. The latter feeling won. The face he saw was a slightly made-up version of Fred. Finally Fred noticed him.

"M! What are you doing *here*?"

"I think I could say the same, Fred"

Fred stepped up to M and greeted him with a wet kiss on the cheek, which took M aback slightly. He had often had bear hugs from Fred the Friendly Dane, but a wet kiss on the cheek? And in make up? Had he become an actor? Was he in drag?

"I'm early for my appointment M, why don't you sit down with me, let's have a little chin-wag"

"Sure, why not indeed?" A small round table by the window had just been vacated. They hurried over.

"I'm meeting my boyfriend, but I'm twenty minutes early – for once. How about you… you okay?"

"Yeah, I was just… walking about. I'm in a bit of a haze I fear. Just had some rather bad news this morning"

"Oh, family?"

"No, closer than that. A friend. Very ill. Probably dying".

"Oh, very sorry to hear that".

"But Fred, listen, I've missed you. Where have you been, what happened? And what do you mean 'boyfriend'?"

There was a big silence. Fred stared at M, as if he was measuring him up for what he might be told.

"There's nothing said about you in the office, you know. Like you never existed. I don't like it. We were good friends Fred. What is going on?"

A look came over Fred's face that reminded M of the last few times he had seen him in the office; his eyes dropped and the whole face sagged. Only the make-up made him look different.

"I'm not at liberty to talk about it M. Let me just say… [heavy sigh]… It was something between Walter and me. Personal matters." He wanted badly to tell M, but he remembered the paper he had signed. He saw his own hand shaping his signature. He was bound, if not legally – he wasn't sure how legal those papers were – then certainly by his honour.

"May I rather tell you something nice?"

"Of course".

"I am quite happy now. Yes *boyfriend!* I've met a really nice boy. Anthony. He went to Oxford, you know. His family is very rich. We're staying in their flat in Knightsbridge. They are totally OK with Tony being gay, and they love the fact that I am Scandinavian. I think they feared he would get an American boyfriend. They're sort of leftie liberals I think. I don't know, don't care about politics. Listen, you *must* come to one of the parties. There's a free flow of *all* substances, if you know what I mean."

M thought he did know what he meant. He sat quiet for a moment, soaking up the change in Fred, the news of his relationship, the implications of the last statement.

"I, I didn't know you were… you know, gay."

Fred threw his head back and laughed.

"Really? I thought everyone realised. You don't approve?"

How could M disapprove. He thought of Isaac. OK, so there's a difference between falling in sin once and choosing to live in it.

Still, the only difference is… the grace of God? The last thought felt hollow and false for M. Like he simply went through the motions of thinking the sort of thoughts he ought to. The truth was he felt happy for Fred. He had seen how unhappy he had been at the church. Now he seemed happy and bubbly again. Why should the correct theology stand in the way of happiness?

"Fred, I am *very* glad for you, if you're happy."

"I am".

Anthony arrived. A tall, slender, dark haired man, with a breezy self confidence that expressed itself in exaggerated politeness and an intense, almost uncomfortable, interest in the other person. M stayed as long as he thought polite without becoming the third wheel, excused himself, and walked back towards Piccadilly Circus. He sauntered aimlessly down to St James' park, where he wandered slowly across the paths observing couples laughing, children running and birds contently floating about on the lake. He felt alone. "If Georg dies," he thought. "Who will understand me?"

In this the children of God are manifest, and the children of the devil: whosoever doeth not righteousness is not of God, neither he that loveth not his brother.

1 JOHN 3; 9 – 10

151

CHAPTER XIV

In which M has more news and learns of The Group of Twelve

Months had passed since the news of Georg's condition; his father had regularly updated him. Told him that Georg had requested certain comics that he liked to read. Hadn't lost his sense of humour, M's father said in an attempt to sound optimistic. M had organised another conference, as well as taking over responsibility for a monthly Holy Communion church service, requiring the coordination of hundreds of volunteers, thousands of chairs to be arranged into small groups, and catering to be supplied for up to fifteen hundred people. The Church board had been impressed with M's organising of it, and his shares were on the rise. Despite the extra hard work, M felt it was worth it. Wasn't church about coming together? Not just sitting in a gigantic hall seeing the back of the neck of the person in front of you, being entertained by a speaker. They had also taken on some more caretakers. Two new Bible College students as part-timers, and an experienced old hand as a full-time caretaker: Dave. When hiring him M had felt he would quickly get into the swing of things. Instead it seemed Dave allowed the swing of things to get to him. He walked in a way that put M in mind of a duck with arthritis. He had very skinny legs, on top of which were planted a torso shaped as a giant pear with matchstick arms sticking out. His head had spiky grey hair and a very long nose that seemed to twitch when he was irritated or frustrated, which was most of the time. He used to come into M's office when he wanted 'advice', which actually meant he wanted to have a bit of a moan. He stood in front of M's desk, hands on hips; pointy elbows sticking out on either side. M thought that he probably looked like what a caretaker would look like in a comedy stage play. He lifted his right arm and stuck one finger in the air, swinging it in a circular motion:

"Look 'ere, M. Oi went to the small 'all to 'oover and there's a group of Afrrricans you know, wanning to have bit of a shandai-marandai prayer meeting, castin' out demons 'n all! I tried to tell 'em oi need to 'oover, but they said they'd booked the meetin' with you?"

M checked on his computer. He had recently computerised the booking system for the various rooms and halls that the church disposed. The meeting *had* been booked.

"Yes, the small hall was booked by Miss Okowalunda's prayer team".

M added that he would make sure the caretakers have an updated printout of the bookings so that they would know who's where when. Somehow this didn't cure Dave's urge to whinge, but it did stop it for the time being, like a little dyke momentarily holding back the flow of muddy water. He stood still. The finger still pointing upwards, taking in this bit of news.

"Yes, yes, that would be verry 'elpful. You're awfully organised there, ain't you M?"

"Thank you, I hope so. Anything else Dave?"

"No… I… er… don't think so. I'll get on with things then, shall oi?"

"Sounds good".

News three:
It was just before the annual January conference, as the first hints of morning

light became evident on a very pale winter sky, that the telephone rang. M opened his eyes and knew immediately what it was about.

"Hello? Oh, hi Tom... Yes, I see... I suppose he is now... When will the funeral be?... I'm not sure to be honest... Of course... Well, thank you for letting me know, Tom... No, no, I was quite awake... Give my regards to your wife and everybody".

And thus ended the short conversation in which M learned that Georg had died.

M felt muted. He took in the information, computed it, filed it in the drawer for 'sad news' and thought of what to wear that day. It was a beautiful, clear winter's morning. The sun shone from its low position over the rooftops as M walked to the train station. People were streaming into the streets, shops were opening, cars passing, there were even some birds singing. It was in every other respect a very lovely day. 'Panta Rei,' thought M. 'Everything flows, as Heraklit said. It all flows on'. One moment is not different from the next, although everything has changed.

The thing that hath been, it is that which shall be; and that which is
done is that which shall be done: and there is
no new thing under the Sun.
ECCLESIASTES I; 9

News four:

Walter had been travelling. He liked to travel. Whenever he went to other churches in other towns and countries he was reminded of how successful he was in their eyes. He especially liked African and South-American churches, as people in these parts of the world still had great reverence for 'The Leader', combined with a deep rooted superstition and mysticism. A latent danger with travelling is, as we all know, that one might pick something up. And at his last trip Walter had indeed picked up something particularly nasty; it was a way of organising the church in groups. Walter had been on a speaking engagement at the Columbian church Corazón Christo, led by the pastor Pedro Sanches. The church had, in the course of only three years, grown from the fairly large size of one thousand members, to the super-size of ten thousand. Everybody who was somebody in the world of charismatic Christianity wanted to be sprinkled with some of Pedro's magic fairy dust. Walter was transfixed by the way they had turned stagnation at a thousand into such seemingly limitless growth. Pastor Pedro willingly explained how God had come to him in a dream, and as with Abraham shown him the stars in the sky and the grains of sand on the beach.

'This is how numerous I will make your church,' God had said, revealing to Pedro the magical way to achieve this growth in membership. Mimic the pyramid structure of network sales organisations, God had said – although not in so many words. This was to be done by establishing a particular type of cell-groups. Now, cell-groups were by no way a new thing in charismatic churches. Indeed, M's home church had practiced cell-groups with considerable failure for years. The concept of cell-groups had been pioneered by the Korean pastor John G. Cho in the '70s and '80s. The idea was to meet in someone's home, making the threshold much lower for the 'unchurched' or non-believer to come along; and as the group slowly but surely grew it would divide, like a cell, and make two groups, which in turn would divide into four groups etcetera, etcetera.

In M's experience the groups had never grown, but rather provided a nice framework for coming together socially once a week, endure an hour or so of Bible reading, a sermon, testimonials and prayers, before enjoying a long evening of tea drinking, waffle eating and music listening.

How is it then, brethren? When ye come together, every one of
you hath a psalm, hath a doctrine, hath a tongue, hath a revelation,
hath an interpretation. Let all things be done unto edifying.
1 CORINTHIANS XIV; 26

The Chelsea Chapel also had a cell-group structure. It was headed up by the Reverend James Carr, and was a fairly lose, bottom-up type of structure. The cell-group leaders had a large degree of freedom to do what they saw fit, and Reverend Carr's work consisted mainly in providing training and pastoral support, and ensuring that the groups by and large stayed 'on message' with what the church was doing at the time. In Columbia, however, they did not believe in such a laissez-faire approach. What Pastor Pedro had done there was to form a group of twelve (himself and eleven disciples), and bid his eleven disciples to gather unto themselves another eleven each, so that every one had a group of twelve. Then the same process was reproduced at the lower level, and so forth down the line in perpetuum, until every church member was in a group. In a country with many poor, uneducated, and superstitious people beholden to hierarchical power structures, the system was a triumph, and Pastor Pedro was the undisputed pharaoh at the top of the pyramid.

When Walter visited and saw what had been achieved, both in terms of the growth of members *and* income, he heard from God that *he* needed to do the same back in London. This strict church structure was a far cry from what had made the Chelsea Chapel great; the loosely knit network of groups and fellowships, catering to the various ethnicities and categories of churchgoers. In addition to Kenyan, Nigerian, Japanese and countless other national groups, there were groups for punks, for the creative types, for the city workers, and the sexual deviants. These, mostly autonomous, groups gave the whole church an anarchic, urbane, happily chaotic flavour in line with the bohemian, multilifestyled way of London. The variety in London is vast: the so-called multiculturalism is baked into one enormous London culture pie, covered and kept cohesively together by a crust of militant toleration.

Now, enticed by the success of Pastor Pedro, Walter wanted to impose the Group of Twelve pyramid-system, not for selling soaps or plastic bowls, but to re-start the growth in membership, that had ground to a halt under his leadership, and thereby also increase the church's revenue; heavily depleted by his insisting on publishing book after book that nobody wanted to buy. There was also another reason: this system, the Group of Twelve, or G12 for short, greatly increased the opportunity for top-down control, which appealed to Walter. Walter repeatedly spoke of the need for the church to be marching to the same drum. It was understood that this was *his* drum. It seemed to Walter that with this organisational structure, a more disciplined approach to church ministry would be within grasp.

M hated the system from the very first second of the very first mention of it. He thought this would be the ruin of the Chelsea Chapel and everything it stood for. And coming from egalitarian Norway he was aghast at the hierarchical nature of the G12-structure, and appalled that the groups would be divided by *gender;* men's groups and women's groups.

There is neither Jew nor Greek, there is neither bond nor free,
there is neither male nor female: for ye are all one in Christ Jesus.
GALATIANS IV; 28

For his own part he felt he had more in common with a Scandinavian woman than an African man. This was like stepping back to the 1950s, he thought, which for Columbians presumably was a great leap forward into modernity. He knew he would resist this with all his might. It would probably last a little while then go away, as so many 'revival' fads he had seen come and go by now. Since they had turned into the third millennium Walter had stopped going on about his 'God-given vision' of '2,000 satellite churches by the year 2000'. It was closer to two *hundred*. M guessed the G12 thing was a way for Walter to divert attention away from his failure to deliver the two thousand satellite churches. But there had also been other, more fleeting phenomena of spiritual revival. When M arrived at Chelsea Chapel, the Sanctification-Revival was in full swing, with scores of church members queuing up to confess publicly to their sins of pornography and general debauchery. It was said to be a preparation for a great revival that would see thousands of non-believers saved and added to the church.

It didn't happen and the fad passed with a lingering flavour of embarrassment. Then there was the oily hands revival. People were reporting that oil inexplicably appeared on their palms and foreheads. But as the summer time passed the oiliness passed also. Then one December people reported magical gold dust to be appearing on their hands and in the air. It was taken as a sign from God, a token of his blessings. Then, as December passed and all the old Christmas decorations were tidied up and the caretakers hoovered and washed the church, somehow the 'gold-dust' ceased to appear. Most bizarrely was perhaps the 'gold tooth revival'. Such was the acceptance that God can do anything, that when reports came in of people allegedly having had gold fillings miraculously put into their teeth, there was a readiness to believe that it was just another way for God to manifest himself.

For M it was a step too far. He could never accept this particular 'revival' as genuine, and was not disappointed when it fizzled out as no one could get hold of a report that could be independently verified by a doctor or dentist. In an indirect acknowledgment that many would expect the G12-initiative to go the way of all the other new fads, Walter had one of the other senior ministers give a talk where he emphatically stated that the G12 'will *not* go away'. M hoped he was wrong, that it *would* blow over and go away. If not, his own going away would have to be considered.

One of the Bible College students they had hired as caretaker in the past half-year was a very good-looking young Swede. After Fred's sudden departure, Walter had been without an apprentice in the office. Then M noticed that the Swede, Johan, when not working in the capacity of caretaker, was carrying Walter's briefcase dressed up in a tight fitting suit and black and white patent shoes. Some time passed, and then Johan informed M that he was quitting as caretaker because Walter wanted him to come and work for him as an assistant in the afternoons after lectures. M was irritated that the Senior Minister's office had not been able to conduct this in a more professional manner.

'How about at least a letter, requesting the transfer, at the very least a courtesy question?' he thought to himself. Of course neither he nor Pete could refuse Walter, but as a matter of form, a token of respect, some sort of formal question should have been posed.

"It would have given us the chance to advertise for a replacement," M said to Mr C who agreed heartily. The good-looking Swede was replaced by Stephan, a nineteen year young South-African Boer with large blue eyes, curly hair and a chiselled, athletic body. He had been heavily into sports back home, but had now come to study the word of God. M and Pete reckoned a sportsman should have the stamina to cope with the hard work of caretaking. Having grown up in the deeply religious, conservative countryside of South Africa, Stephan was ill prepared for the in-your-face perversity of Londoners. Waiting for the bus he was approached by a man who asked him which way he swung. He hadn't realised what the question was about. Another man came up and asked where he'd been all his life. Stephan told M about these crude chat-up lines with an expression of deep shock and horror. There was an air of naïvety about Stephan, struggling to keep his head above the cynical whirlwind of the big sinful city.

In the old, non air-conditioned building of Chelsea Chapel, the overcrowded Sundays in August could be sheer torture, especially for Mr C who had a propensity to perspire easily and copiously. He and M had escaped to the room behind the reception, where some cool air could be had, as the service was going full steam ahead with loud music, singing and clapping.

"It's a wonder the old building doesn't collapse," thought M.

"Make us a cuppa M, will you?" said Pete.

"Of course" replied M.

"Make it so strong that the spoon stands up in it, he-he-he" said Pete, as he always did when he asked for tea.

"They say drinking a warm drink cools you down, but I'm not sure if I believe it", M remarked.

As they sat and sipped their brew and chatted, Stephan came in hesitantly, looking very pale and sweaty. He nodded to his superiors, then turned and went back into the reception. Pete and M looked at each other, M went over to the door and called him back in the office. Stephan, who was normally all smiles, had an ashen cloud hanging over his countenance.

"Stevie! Come on in. Have a cup of tea, won't you?"

"No, I'm OK thank you."

"What's the matter Stephan?"

Stephan looked thoughtful and pensive. "Well…no!"

"What?"

By this time Pete had become curious too.

"Steve, my boy! Come in here!"

Stephan shuffled his short legs into the back-office again.

Pete gave him his stern hangdog look: "What's the matter Steven?"

Stephan had a look of agony on his face.

"It's just… no I cawn't say it", he said in his plaintive Afrikaans accent.

M put his hand on Stephan's shoulder.

"Come on Stephan. You can tell us, whatever it is".

Stephan struggled a bit with his inhibition, then finally decided it was better out than in.

"I was on duty to clean the toilets, change the toilet paper and all that"

"Yes…?"

The look in Stephan's eyes made M and Pete imagine all sorts of things one might discover in a public loo. They imagined the headlines in the redtop tabloids.

Continued Stephan: "I had just changed the toilet paper in the middle cubicle when I noticed something written on the wall in black mawrker pen."

"What?" said his seniors in unison.

"It said… no I don't know if I can say it."

"Oh go on for goodness sake", said Pete, who was growing impatient.

"It said… *'Walter is gay'*". He seemed at once deeply ashamed and relieved at having relayed this statement. He looked from Mr C to M and back with his big, blue, guilty looking eyes.

A few seconds of absolute silence befell M and Pete as they realised that this was all. Then, as if on cue, they both started laughing, and had to put hand to mouth so as not to be heard in the church hall. Stephan stood looking confused, trying guiltily to smile too. Was it funny? Not shockingly serious? Wiping a tear from his eye M put his hand back on Stephan's shoulder.

"Sorry to laugh, it's *just…* the look on your face". Pete started laughing again and M joined in.

"No, no, seriously" tried Pete. "We need to get it cleaned off you know. Call Francis!"

M called the Frenchman who entered shortly after.

"Francis!" Pete had an accusatory way of barking Francoise's name that made the Frenchman take an apologetic attitude, just in case.

"Yes Pete, 'ow may I 'elp you?"

"Francis, someone has done something on the wall of a toilet cubicle"

Francoise looked aghast. "Oo la la! Oh mah Godd, dat is, how-you-say, disgusteeng!"

M realised what Francoise thought.

"No, no, it's not quite as bad as *that*. Someone has written, 'Walter is gay' on a wall, in marker pen."

"Door, actually," interjected Stephan.

Francoise's face went through several changes. It looked laughing, then as if relishing something, then mock horror, then serious: "Oh mah godd. Oo la la, he! We must take it away! At once!"

"Yes Francis" said Pete. "Have you got that stuff o' yours?"

Francoise found his graffiti remover, and he rushed down to the toilets with Pete and Stephan close at heel.

M felt the need for a bit of fresh air – or London air at any rate. He went out to the front step overlooking the church car park, surrounded by trees. He thought of how sad it was for Walter to have to go through his life denying who and what he was. Denying a part of his self. Being *self*-less. That is the ideal, isn't it? To not have a self. But how can you value things, other people, the world, your own life, if you don't value your *self* first?

Thou shalt love thy neighbour as thyself.
MARK XII; 31

He then thought how he abhorred the G12 structure. He had been placed in a group with people he didn't know nor care about, but for whom it was his duty to care. It made him dislike both the duty and the people. Believers often say that even if God in the end turns out not to exist they would have lived a better life for being Christians. How could this be if it meant denial of what makes you you? Of what you are? It was his faith, the belief that he had been called there that kept him at the Chelsea Chapel and in a system that he was increasingly unhappy with. M had booked some time off, and would be spending ten days in the hometown. He hoped it would give him some time to think.

CHAPTER XV

In which our hero visits his hometown and has a conversation

It was very strange to return to the old hometown again. Especially now that Georg was not there. As the airport shuttle-bus entered the town centre he saw the familiar buildings under the dark grey sky. He recognised people who were still wearing the same coats as when he left. It felt as if time had stood still, yet so much had changed in M's world. His father picked him up from town and as they drove home his father told him in great detail about the old Mercedes estate he had bought and was in the process of restoring. M thought about Georg.

His mother welcomed him with hugs and tears and his favourite dinner. His older brother was there too. M took out the cognac and cigarettes he had brought, and the evening passed with the slight elation of spirit that coming together after absence can produce. It is the feeling of almost being strangers who have to become acquainted, yet the bond of familiarity lies invisibly behind it all and makes it slightly more relaxed and informal – yet with some unspecified expectations unspoken of, and more often than not unmet. It is a pleasant state that only lasts for a little while. At some point in the evening M thought it would have been time for him to pop over to Georg's. But there was no Georg to pop over to.

The next morning was Sunday. M's old church, Happy Life, had relocated to cheaper rooms. They'd had to in recent years, as membership had dwindled. M went along not knowing what to expect. The service was a subdued affair. The energy and drive that once had been a magnet for young people and a reinvigorating force for the not so young had dissipated. Instead of the electrical guitar, keyboard and bass, supported by Georg's steady drumming; a lone guitar player led the singing with some flaccid hippie hymns. It was as if all the anti-religious zeal and zest had gone out of them, and they had accepted their place as simply a variety of religiosity. They had not the pipe organ and the high altar, but they were no better than the Lutheran church in their habitual procedures and sacramental ceremonies. M knew he no longer belonged. He looked around and saw people he used to love and care about but who he was no longer particularly interested in. After the service he stayed for coffee. Since Sigmund's departure the position of pastor had been divided between Mary and Harry. Mary was a highly strung lady in her forties, who, when she spoke publicly, channelled her deep-routed nervousness with full force into the bottle neck of an unnaturally strained, shouty voice; becoming redder and redder in the face as she went on. Some thought that this was the power of the Spirit upon her. M thought it was creepy. Harry was totally different. He was a skinny man with mouse grey hair in his early fifties, with a photographic memory and no imagination. He spoke publicly with an apologetic smile on his lips, and a charming speech impediment that made him pronounce 'r' the manner of a Frenchman. Harry was one of those optimists you could depend upon always to be in a good mood, ready with a smile and an encouraging comment. He had a slightly high-pitched, whiny voice, and would punctuate his sentences with a strangely nervous laughter.

"Good to see you again M," said Harry, slapping M's shoulder lightly, in a friendly sort of way.

"Thank you Harry, nice to see the old gang again," half lied M. "Although, it is very strange to be back and not have Georg here".

"Yes, well, he's in a better place now," said Harry. The old cliché irritated M.

"That may be so, but he didn't *want* to die, you know. He was too young".

The days of our years are threescore years and ten;
and if by reason of strength they be fourscore years
PSALM 90; 10

"Heh-heh, yes, of course, that is so, but you know, where he is now he is much happier. Heh-heh. No suffering, you know". Harry had a slightly worried look on his face.

"Yeah, yeah, I know all that, Harry. You know I know. But still, Georg didn't *want* to die. He wasn't ready for it. He wanted to go on living *here on earth;* to play his drums, listen to his jazz, drink his tea and… all that," M trailed off as he realised none of this meant very much to Harry.

"Yes, heh-heh, well, but you know he is playing his drums now in a much better place."

M gave up. At the back of his mind was the belief, so strongly held and loudly preached a few years back: that healing belonged to the believer. That Christ's redemptive work meant not only salvation for the soul, but also healing for the body. This, they used to say, was a teaching of the Bible forgotten by the established churches. Happy Life was part of the worldwide movement of reformist revival Christianity that would restore the early church's true Christian doctrine and practice. Healing by prayer was to become an integral part of the church services, just like prayer for anything else. But M did not at that moment see any purpose in confronting Harry with the fact that if they had really believed in physical healing then Georg's body should have been healed. The comfort of "a better place" was the established church's way of talking.

And Peter, fastening his eyes upon him with John, said, Look on us.
And he gave heed unto them, expecting to receive
something of them.
Then Peter said, Silver and gold have I none; but such as I have
give I thee: In the name of Jesus Christ of Nazareth rise up and walk.
And he took him by the right hand, and lifted him up: and
immediately his feet and ankle bones received strength.
And he leaping up stood, and walked, and entered with them into
the temple, walking, and leaping, and praising God.
ACTS III; 4 – 8

'What has happened to them?' thought M. 'They have lost the fire. The Prometheus of revivalist Christianity had been drenched by a shower of cold reality. For Harry it was perhaps easy to fall back on the traditional notion of a better by-and-by. He had worked his entire adult life in a routine factory job. For him church meant an exciting and pleasant break from the drudgery of his everyday existence. To escape this earth would be a marvellous promotion. For M it was yet another example of the pick 'n' mix Christianity that he deplored. 'You either believe it all, or nothing,' he thought. 'These people look away from the unpleasant facts.' But M himself still looked away from perhaps the most unpleasant thought of all. 'No, somehow it all started, though,' he thought to himself. 'Something cannot come of nothing'.

Perhaps he could believe in a sort of Aristotelian first mover, the God of the Enlightenment thinkers: a cosmic watchmaker who winds everything up and then sits back. M *wanted* to believe in God, but the idea seemed increasingly distant, ungraspable, pointless. He looked around him. Some of the old gang were still there, but without Georg they seemed like planets without a point of gravity around which to revolve. They were pointless. M had seen them through a prism of joint understanding with Georg, he had placed them in relation to Georg. There was Olaf who was ten years older than M, unmarried, still living with his mother, highly intelligent but suffering from schizophrenia. Olaf was defined in relation to Georg by two key characteristics: Firstly; when they ate waffles, Georg would always divide the waffles into six equally big pieces and apply butter, sour cream and jam on each one equally. Olaf on the other hand would smear everything on his waffle, fold it over and eat the whole thing in a messy and indecorous manner. Whenever they had waffles Georg and M would exchange looks, Georg turning his eyes upwards in a slightly exasperated expression. What would be the point of having waffles with Olaf if there was no Georg to exchange looks with. Secondly; Olaf did not appreciate the comic strips of *Calvin and Hobbes*. This was a serious flaw. Even as Georg lay in hospital, dying, and M's father visited him and asked if he could bring him something, Georg had asked for some *Calvin and Hobbes* comics. But when M and he discussed the subtleties of the warm humour Olaf assumed an overbearing countenance. It meant that Planet Olaf orbited slightly further from the point of gravity. Then there was Tom, who was a year younger than M. He was also defined against the Georgian ideal by two main points.

Firstly, aesthetics; almost unfathomable to Georg and M, Tom liked country music! Of course, Tom would emphasize repeatedly, it was the 'high quality' and more genuinely folksy *bluegrass country*. And indeed Georg could tolerate certain Emmylou Harris tracks, just as Tom had to tolerate the streams of jazz pouring forth from Georg's stereo. But then Tom also fell asleep during Bergman films, and had great difficulty with other arty films that Georg and

M insisted on watching. Tom preferred *Friends*. Georg and M could tolerate *Friends* but preferred *Seinfeld*.

Secondly, The Speed of Eating; if Georg had a chocolate, he would unwrap it carefully, smoothing out the wrapping paper so that if would form a square surface from which to serve it (if this was not possible due to the nature of the wrapping paper he would invariably obtain a plate of some sort). He would then take a knife and divide the chocolate into several equally sized bites, offer to others and then proceed to eat the chocolate very slowly. One particularly vulgar young woman in the church who had once witnessed this process, had laughed and scoffed loudly at what she saw as the niggliness of it. It had defined her as belonging to another solar system altogether. Tom would unwrap, and holding the chocolate with the wrapping paper, wolf it down in two bites. Without fail, Georg would turn and look at Tom, raising his eyebrows disapprovingly and in mock surprise at the speed of consumption. Tom would look sheepish and say, "I was hungry". They would reply, "you're always hungry", and then they would all laugh as if in a sitcom. M had himself been a bit of a wolfer. His whole family was very fond of food, and ate fast and without moderation.

On the last day of school before holidays (and *only* on that day) teachers would allow children to bring in a bottle of fizzy drinks, biscuits and a bag of crisps. Almost all the children brought a small bottle, the classic 300ml glass bottles of coke being typical, a small packet of crisps, one tiny chocolate and dry biscuits without cream. M's mother would pack with him a litre bottle of coke, a huge family pack of crisps, a giant chocolate and the creamiest biscuits on the market: *French Waffles*. The teachers laughed and the children admired M's supreme tuck supply. No doubt the indulgence insulated M from the social-democratic neo-puritan guilt of Norwegian society, but from Georg's example M learned voluntary moderation, and only bought the larger sizes in order to share.

Attending a supper with his friends from the church later that day, he could not shake the feeling of loss. He looked around at them. There was no point in any of these people now that he could not define them against the one who was gone.

Back in London M became convinced Pete had suffered some sort of breakdown. He didn't realise it straight away. A number of incidents pointed to it. One otherwise grey day M entered Pete's office to find him leafing through papers engrossed in buoyant conversation with the reverend John Carr, the former Church of England minister who had become the head of the cell-group division in the Chelsea Chapel and Metropolitan Church Network. Unusually for Pete he was sitting in his lounge area, on the easy chair, with John on the settee.

"Ah M, come in, come in, dear boy," Pete beckoned, his steel-rimmed reading glasses halfway down his nose.

M took a seat. Pete and James eyed him silently, smiling like two naughty schoolboys.

"What's up then?" asked M, as he poured himself a coffee.

Pete removed his reading glasses.

"How would you like to go to Berlin and set up an office with me?"

M laughed.

"What? Berlin? What's that all about then?"

Pete leaned forward and said in a lowered voice. "Well, I'm in talks, all hush-hush at the moment, with the Bernhard Hinne Ministry. They are looking to set up a European office in Berlin, and if it comes off I will need an office manager to run the administrative side of things." He leaned back again. "How about that?"

M couldn't help smiling. He took pleasure in being 'wanted', in being so much in demand that Pete was prepared to steal him away. James Carr kept smiling. The reverend James Carr is not all that easy to describe. Just over medium height, with a sort of medium bulky body, giving him a deceptively cuddly appearance. His head stood up from his shoulders not as a round thing on top of a neck, but as a coned continuation of the upper body, a soft bullet sprinkled with a wreath of short, blond-grey hair. He had small, twinkling, grey-blue eyes and a thin lipped mouth curled up in a little naughty smile, like a misbehaving schoolboy – or perhaps more like one taking pleasure in other boys' misbehaviour. Carr was a proper minister. He had studied theology and gone into the ministry in the Church of England. He had maneuvered himself to a London diocese and gradually found himself gravitating towards the charismatic faction of the church. His great hobbyhorse was cell-groups, around which he had built his reputation; achieving attendance growth at his C of E congregation in a time of steady decline all around. It was this cell-group fame that had brought him to be 'headhunted' by the Chelsea Chapel, as Walter saw the potential for growth that his satellite-system had failed to produce. From the very first day he met him, M had noticed there was something a little different about James. For a start he wore slippers in the office. Then there was the interior decoration of his office. The offices at Chelsea Chapel where unified only by the theme of 'waste not; want not'. Old desks and office chairs in a multitude of shapes and colours that had been accumulated over time were interspersed with scruffy filing cabinets and over-filled boxes, and an array of computers and printers – all different models, sizes and shapes – were placed on these various desks and tables, creating an impression of a car-boot sale; in a sense quite appropriate for the offices of a frugal charity. However much one tried to tidy and clean, though, a slightly gloomy look of impersonal scruffiness remained. James was given a medium sized office, only three doors down from Walter's, previously occupied by a member of the pastoral staff who had, as so many others, failed to come back after a period of sick leave. Pete had told M to have the old hand-me-down desk and cabinets in this office removed for James' coming, and when he moved in the caretakers carried up box after box of stuff to go in there. When M saw the result he thought it looked like the territory of a different country: a brand new desk (or so at least it seemed) in light beech, a high-back black leather chair, IKEA-bookshelves in same colour as desk, kitted out with actual books, framed pictures and decorative knickknacks, a little visitor's table with two easy chairs, pictures and diplomas on the wall, and a carpet on the floor. It actually looked homely. For the visitor the effect was *trust*. One felt the reassurance of a soft sanctuary, an intimate zone, a hushed harbour. Combined with James having been a proper priest in a robe, this gave the visitor the confidence to open up, spill any tinned up beans and confess. M wondered later whether it was a conscious ploy by Walter to have a pastors' pastor for the staff to go to, as he was somewhat unapproachable himself. What M did eventually discover was that the atmosphere of confessionary trust was honoured more in the breach than in the observance: Reverend James was a bit of a mole. Inducing people, by his, sometimes irreverent jokes and impudent comments, to come out with what they *really* thought and felt about Walter, for them later to be frozen out from Walter's confidence. But at the time that M returned from Norway to find James and Pete in buoyant mood, talking about Berlin, James was the trusted go-to man for Pete to unburden his frustrations. Pete had known James since long before he came to the Chelsea Chapel, when organising events for Jacob Cherubo. Having grown up with a father who was a pastor, Pete's instinctive trust in pastors was as strong as his acquired distrust of preachers. Walter was a *preacher*, James was a *pastor*. When James preached a sermon he never became 'preachy'. He spoke in a quietly authoritative way, like a wise father giving his considered opinion, interspersed with some rehearsed jokes and icebreakers. When he spoke to parishioners he had a caring tone of voice, where Walter was sourly didactic. M thought he sounded slightly patronizing, but he also admired the professionalism in James' change from impish colleague to sensible priest; although the hint of insincerity in it made M slightly uncomfortable. Nothing came of the German plan. Instead M noticed that Pete was spending more and more time with Sara Grühn, after promoting her to head of the Media Division of the church.

Around this time there was surprising news. The surly Arthur Kentworthy, Walter's Executive Assistant who had reacted so humourlessly to M's caricature comic, was leaving. Arthur had fallen in love with a blond Dutch lady with bright, blue eyes, and large, white teeth, almost constantly bared in smile. Her sunny countenance had a marked positive influence on Arthur; he smiled more and looked happy and relaxed. Arthur had recently bought a two bedroom terraced house in a suburb to the west of London. Now it was revealed that he and his fiancé were planning to move to Holland as soon as they were married, and so he needed to let his house. M relished the idea of living in a house with a garden. He arranged to share it with a Bible College student who had been a fellow in the first year, and who had gone on to do the second year, and due to the reasonable price it came out no more expensive than renting a much smaller place in central London.

For Walter the loss of Arthur was unwelcome. Arthur had been an efficient enforcer, a dutiful buffer between Walter and the rest of the staff, an eminently able business manager. M had expected Pete to start working closer with Walter. Instead Walter decided to promote Charlie Hatkinson, who was already among the senior pastoral staff, to the role of main pastor for the old church, and second in command to Walter for the whole city church. He also decided to bring his wife, Angela, more closely into the day-to-day business of the church. As far as M could observe, Pete seemed if anything to be moving further away from Walter. There had been small signs that worried M. More often than not

Pete wore a harried look on his face when M saw him together with Sara. Then one weekend Pete's wife Maggie came up to town. Maggie was a formidable lady. Of the same height as her husband with a certain solidity of build, she had a square face decorated with a pair of large square glasses framing a pair of weary, cynical eyes. Pete had remarked more than once that there was one person Walter seemed to fear, and that was Maggie. She saw straight through him, penetrated the superficial nonsense with her commonsensical clear sight. On Sunday afternoons, between services, Pete often invited M to join him for lunch.

Sometimes they would be a whole group of people. Pete would always choose a restaurant in the upper level of quality and price, and he would always pay for M. It made M wonder how much Pete actually earned. This Sunday M was also invited to join Pete and Maggie for lunch. But instead of an expensive restaurant they went to a cheap buffet pizza joint. It was the sort of establishment people go to who don't like pizza. Thick, soft, half-baked dough covered with ketchup and plastic cheese. The ice cream came out of a tap and landed in the cup looking like white turd, tasting like artificial milk. Was something going on with Pete's economy? M had also noticed that rather than going to his normal expensive perfumier, Pete had gone to Boots and bought a middle of the range cologne. Stranger still was it that Sara did not come to eat with them. She worked very closely with Pete, but that weekend she was nowhere to be seen. There had been some lose talk about the two of them. M found it ridiculous that anyone could think that young, slim, good-looking Sara would be interested in a man like Pete. M had informed Pete of the comment, partly out of dutiful loyalty, and partly because he didn't like the person who had passed the comment to him. Nevertheless, Pete seemed to use any excuse to have a meeting with Sara, she was always in his office, or he in hers.

He had her promoted, and although she became increasingly out of her depth, Pete kept giving her more and more responsibility. It was not what she wanted nor needed. She had done so well as head of the Bookshop, but now as head of the entire Media Division and with Pete's increasing demands on her, the elasticity was being stretched. M remembered meeting her in the staff kitchen where she proceeded to spew out her frustrations with the church leadership in a long, incoherent rant, whilst frantically washing some dishes in running water. She used running water, she explained apologetically, due to her fear of germs. M kept nodding sympathetically, whilst thinking she was a bit strange.

Pete popped his head through the door to M's office one lunchtime and asked if he needed to buy any supplies for church from the superstore down the road. M did have a list of things they needed.

"Well come with me then" said Pete. "I need to do some shopping too".

As they walked down the corridor Reverend James met them with his coat on. James wore his boyish, naughty smile. It was the same smile he used to have when he came to M to request stationery.

"Let's go on a spending spree", he would say, before signing his own purchase order (which, as a Divisional Head, he could). As they entered the superstore, Pete sped along in front with a large trolley and was lost in a labyrinth of groceries.

James inclined his head towards M, "you know he's shopping for Sara, don't you?"

"Oh really?" M pretended not to have guessed.

"Yes, apparently she's not feeling well, and Pete volunteered to do her shopping for her".

"Oh well, that's very kind, isn't it?"

James laughed. "Yes, very kind indeed".

M disliked James' gossipy way of talking about his colleagues and brethren in Christ. Like his father, M didn't like to talk about his own matters with others or about other people's matter with a third party. His father had tried to make his wife understand this, as she brought home the pickings of the day's gossip foraging.

"I don't *want* to know," he would say. "It's none of my concern and not yours either".

But female communication seems to depend on delving into and sympathizing with one another's problems, and mapping out where the various females stand in the hierarchy of the female pecking order. M's mother could no more stop gossiping than stop breathing, but, unlike many other women, she drew the line at criticizing her husband to outsiders. M therefore came to see gossiping as something weak and female. Something ladies did over a cup of coffee and cakes. Men discussed proper issues, such as politics, the economy, cars and music. James' gossipy talk made him, in M's eyes, a bit of an old lady.

For every kind of beasts, and of birds, and of serpents, and of things
in the sea, is tamed, and hath been tamed of mankind:
but the tongue can no man tame;
it is an unruly evil, full of
deadly poison.
... Out of the same mouth proceedeth blessing and cursing.
JAMES III; 5 – 10

Chapter XVI

In which Charlie takes charge, and we meet a lady with sensible shoes

After taking up his new responsibilities Charlie Hatkinson went through a metamorphosis. From cheeky chappie, always with a glint in the eye and a joke at the ready, to a psychopathic version of David Brent. Trying to be managing director of an organisation far too large and unwieldy for someone with no previous managerial experience or training. From day one he was drowning – his desperation and fear hidden behind a darkening face. The divisional heads had no real respect for him, and Walter wanted him simultaneously to be sycophantically obsequious and effectively managerial like Arthur Kentworthy had been. Charlie attempted this by becoming more and more unreasonable towards the divisional heads and managerial staff. M felt it by an increasing demand for written reports on all sorts of minutiae. Pete felt it by having his access to Walter practically stopped. If he sent Walter a memo it would come back with, 'see Charlie about it'. Everything now had to go through Charlie. A memo arrived telling Pete his responsibility for personnel matters would be taken away and given to Angela, Walter's wife. Then Charlie informed him that he would have to move out of the church's property, a small, basement flat where Pete had been staying during the week.

It had been a semi grace-and-favour arrangement, but the age of grace and favours was quickly running out. Pete's scope of decision-making power was reduced week by week. Sara, who had been on sick leave a while didn't come back, with no one mentioning it.

Then Charlie decreed that all staff-members had to have a G12-group. Pete needed to create a group consisting of the departmental heads of his division; M, Ben Carton, Diego Hezpionsa, and a couple of other departmental heads within Operations, would meet one morning a week with pastries and coffee to make it as much a social occasion as a spiritual one. Men may not live by bread alone, but it helps.

But each of the departmental heads also had to have a group. M held back for as long as he could, but eventually he was assigned three people and instructed to meet them every Sunday after the 11 o'clock service. The group consisted of Daniel, fresh from Trinidad and Tobago. He seemed to be an amalgamation of African and Asian genes: large, beautiful, dark eyes, small nose, large mouth with huge, white teeth, and with the insecurity of someone who knows he doesn't quite understand the culture he has landed in. There was a sweet innocence in his demeanour that London would quickly disabuse him of. Next was Jim, a white – or rather ashen-grey – English man in his mid-40s or possibly early 50s. He had a depleted, sunken appearance, and spoke in a low, insecure voice. He seemed totally devoid of self-confidence. M felt that as meaningless as the whole G12-structure appeared to him, perhaps he could make it worthwhile by trying to help Jim. The last member was Jack from Australia, a tallish twenty something with blond-red hair, a freckled, pale face sporting a large, pointy nose and grey, untrustworthy eyes. He also had the manners of a dog that obeys another master. He wore a facial expression of bland, unsmiling earnestness that irritated M and reminded him of a boy scout ready to earn himself brownie points by pointing out the mistakes of others.

To ensure that all joy was removed from the G12-group, Charlie had sheets printed up with the points of discussion at the meeting, which were distributed to all G12-groups that met in the church on a Sunday. M pretended he had forgotten to bring it, but to his utter annoyance Jack had remembered to pick up an extra copy.

"Ah, thank you," M said, and paid some lip service to it, before he veered off on his own route.

Having a paper telling you what to talk about went right against the grain of the Christianity M had grown up with in Pastor Sigmund's church. There, the leading principle had been to use your own spiritual ability to be sensitive to what God would have you say; to be inspired by the Spirit of God to serve up the special Word He had for you that day. M looked at poor Jim, and felt he wanted to at least try and help *him*, if he could. He mustered the memory of all the American-style, positive, self-motivational scriptures that Sigmund had fed him with in previous years. And by the end of the session he thought he saw a spark deep in Jim's sad eyes. The next Sunday M took the instruction sheet and demonstrably folded it in front of his group.

"Today, I feel the Lord is leading me in a different direction".

He enjoyed seeing the look of fear and confusion on Jack's face. Daniel looked mildly questioning, but recognised the way of speaking. Jim simply looked spiritually hungry. M inserted the virtual spout into Jim's soul and poured down the power-feed of concentrated self-confidence boosting proteins, he fed him condensed guilt-redemption, and sprinkled his spiritual corn flakes with affirmations of his value; that *he* can make a real difference. That God would never ask more of you than that He knows you can manage; perhaps all you were asked to do was to smile at someone, to spread a little cheer. M noticed that Jim seemed to sit up more. At the first meeting he sat bowed, looking deflated. Now he gradually reflated, as he seemed to realise that God was looking for ways, not to punish him, but simply to *use* him and bless him.

Jim started showing up in smarter clothes. He seemed to go from grey-scale to being in colour. His manners were more open and he contributed readily. Daniel also appeared more confident and open than he had seemed in the beginning. Jack was the odd one out. He always had a slightly worried look on his face when M calmly folded the instruction sheet away and followed his own prepared notes. After a few weeks – in which M had to admit to himself that he enjoyed this group-thing more than he wanted to – he had a call from Charlie to come and see him in his office. M knocked on the door, and instead of an instant 'come in' he was left to wait for a tangible length of time. 'Pretentious little twat.' thought M generously, before the 'come in' finally was heard through the door and M entered. Charlie sat behind a desk that seemed far too large for him, like David in Saul's armour. The difference with this David, though, was that far from being prepared to take it off, he pathetically kept staggering around in it.

"Come in, have a seat," he said without looking up from some papers. M sat down and waited again. Finally Charlie looked up and forced a smile.

"So, how's the G12-group going?"

M winced a little at the mention of G12, realising he was actually taking part in it. He replied he thought it was not going at all too bad. Charlie's face theatrically changed to a more serious, frowny expression.

"Now, you understand of course that we want the G12-groups to be... what shall we say... an *integral* part of the church, yes?"

"Why, naturally!" M said disingenuously.

"So, it is important that the various group leaders are... *in tune* with what the pastor, or the speaker, is saying". He looked expectantly at M.

"Yes, I am sure that's very important," M replied flatly.

Charlie shifted a little in his chair, then went on impatiently:

"Well, do you find the sheets we hand out helpful?"

The penny dropped with a loud Australian clang.

"Of course it is *most* helpful to know what the leadership wants to emphasise".

"Right, so it is really important to *use* it". He leaned forward and looked at M. "I do suppose you use the sheet in your group?"

It was M's turn to shift a little in the chair.

"Oh, I always keep it with me, and of course refer to it". That was true. He always took it with him, and always folded it up. He also referred to it as 'that bloody nonsense', but he didn't see the need to go into this level of specificity.

Charlie wrung his hands and frowned in a mock-worried way.

"Well, because, it is just that I happened to meet one of your group members, and he just mentioned in passing that you don't always... take the sheet quite as seriously as perhaps we ought to".

At this M wanted to burst out laughing. He had won. They could demand that he works Sundays. They could tell him to take a group. They could even instruct him to use a sheet, but they couldn't make him take it seriously. Disguising his giggles with a cough he tried to look offended.

"Of course I take it seriously. I may add the odd point where I feel led by the Spirit, but the framework is still... you know, the sheet gives the frame, and the emphasis".

Charles sat back, happy to have had this concession from M. Satisfied that he had made M lie a little bit to hide what he was really doing, if for no other reason but that it meant M was taking some sort of ownership of the group and might in time come fully on-board the G12-vision. M looked at the smug face below the shiny hair and wished he could hate Charlie. But instead he felt only pity for him. And those you pity you soon despise, and those you despise cannot truly lead you. A good leader is one you want to imitate. There was nothing about Charlie, or Walter for that matter, M wanted to imitate. And less was to come.

In their attempt to be free, non-religious, led by the Spirit of God – as opposed to the dead liturgical procedures in the established church – the services at Chelsea Chapel were full of rhetoric about wind, fire and being led by the spirit.

For as many as are led by the Spirit of God, they are the sons of God.
ROMANS VIII; 15

But the only real outward difference from a High-Church Anglican service was the absence of the pipe-organ; they had an electrically amplified worship band, apart from that they were as strictly formulaic as any ritual based church, only according to a different formula. The worship-band would strike up a couple of upbeat songs for all to join in. Then the leader of the meeting (mostly Charlie) would welcome everyone, and lead in a prayer. Another song. Then serious words, with quotes from the Bible on the importance of giving your tithes and offerings. A slow, sentimental song as the collection buckets were passed, then practical information and announcements, followed by a solo-number by one of the church singers, in preparation for the speaker (mostly Walter). Walter normally preferred an upbeat, joyful song to precede his speaking, but occasionally he would whisper in the ear of Willy Booth, the leader of the worship group and administrative head of the Music Department, that he wanted a soft song. The song would gradually turn into a protracted prayer session – people standing swaying with eyes closed and arms raised, their critical senses gradually dissipating into a state of suggestive receptiveness.

M had led the choir in the home church, as well as playing in a band together with Georg. The inspiration for the choir M led, was unusual for Norwegian church choirs: M had been able to get hold of reels and cassette tapes with recordings from the revival that swept the USA in the 1950s and 60s. The poor audio quality was made up for by the energetic intensity, the effervescent frabjousity, the fracas and hooping, the clapping and anarchistic choir singing, which appealed strongly to M. It was the absolute antithesis to the overly polished, nice, white gospel choirs, so popular with the European audiences. Georg and M listened attentively to wobbly recordings of the big names in American revivalist history, most notably the 'reverend' A.A. Allen, the first white preacher to have a mixed race choir on stage. At his height Allen traversed the US with a huge circus tent and performed his revival act to tens, possibly hundreds, of thousands of people. There were alleged healings, demon-expulsions and dramatic conversions – lifted to ecstatic elevation by the music and singing. Allen himself ended his life in the ignominy of pill and alcohol abuse, which he apparently fell into due to the excruciating pain in his back brought on by an injury God stubbornly refused to heal him of. Notwithstanding, the recordings gave M an impossible ideal for his church music.

Unfortunately, the choir-members, musicians and churchgoers hadn't heard these old recordings, and it was very difficult to make them reproduce the energy, joyfulness and madness of the old campground meetings. But try M did. He had a good voice, and was able, with Georg and the band, to reproduce some of the exuberance of the old-fashioned black church music.

When he arrived at the Chelsea Chapel Bible College, M discovered one who shared his dislike of contemporary Christian music: Charlie Hatkinson. During the obligatory worship session in the morning before lectures, the music-leader Willy Booth, from his large electronic keyboard, would lead the congregated students in anodyne songs that lacked the sound theological intelligence of the classic hymns, and had nothing of the raw energy of the black American church music. The black church music derived its joy from a deep and strong sense of revelation; of the theology of liberation from oppression and servitude – the Hebrews versus the Egyptians; the slaves versus the slave-keepers; the sinners versus Satan – expressed with an ecstatic intensity of emotion borne from an understanding that permeated body and soul that this was real. It was a matter of life and death, not just a lifestyle choice. It was for them not a matter of picking the religion that 'worked for you', but of eternal redemption or eternal damnation; it was absolute conviction – and M loved it. Willy Booth's joyfulness, on the other hand, smacked more of the frantic, artificial cheeriness of children's TV presenters. It had no depth – there was no struggle behind it, at least nothing more taxing than finding a parking spot for the Volvo. As had become his habit around this time, M mixed himself a strong instant coffee and went into the adjacent hall to escape the faux jollity. In the shadow stood Charlie Hatkinson, the lecturer of the day. He stepped out of the darkness and looked at M conspiratorially, "do you also dislike Willy's music?" he asked with a naughty half smile and a twinkle in the eye.

M had been a little taken aback by the frankness but confirmed.

"I generally do not like any of the modern hymns and church-songs," then went on to explain about his discovery of black revivalist music from the 1950s, and found that Charlie also had a strong interest in the period's preaching and music.

He was also a great fan of Elvis Presley. M felt good about finding a confederate in his music taste at that level in the church. When it transpired that M had led worship in his home church he was asked to go on the roster for leading the morning worship in college. Having introduced some of the old revivalist songs, the word spread to Walter who gave the green light for M to be included on the list of church singers for the main services. M would with regular intervals perform the solo number. On these days he would arrive at 7am on a Sunday, do his operational duties first, then before the service change into a gold-colour silk shirt and patent leather shoes, and wow the congregation with his rapturous songs, quick-stepping dance movements, and unbounded joyfulness. Occasionally he invited a little, old, black lady onto the stage to do a little knees-up dance with him. It was raucous, it was fun, it was extremely efficient and popular. The congregation loved him, and M genuinely loved them back. M had many doubts throughout his Christian walk. Intellectual questions and logical difficulties that were hard to reconcile. But he really believed that when he stepped on to that stage and gave his absolute all and a bit, pouring his entire soul and spirit into his performance, he was being more honest and more *anointed* by God than at any other area in his life. He saw the look of joy and encouragement on the face of the people. He, or rather God through him, gave people real happiness.

O clap your hands, all ye people;
shout unto God with the voice of triumph.
PSALMS 47; 1

Occasionally, if Willy Booth was away, M would be asked to lead the main worship music. M did this in the same black church music way that he did his solo numbers, which, in the predominately black church, went down very well indeed. M sensed that when he led the worship, people had a shock and surprise; that worshipping God could be fun, and yet deeply felt. It was as if they had a pent up need for expressing joy that didn't find an outlet in the normal European style of contemporary worship music. When M let loose the old-fashion revivalists songs the congregation erupted in such an explosion of clapping, dancing, shouting, singing that even he was surprised at the effect his music was having.

One particular Sunday, after M had led the worship music and was standing in the room behind the stage panting from the physical exertion, Charlie caught up with him.

"Oh M, a quick word please"

"Of course," gasped M, sweating.

Charlie's face was expressionless. He had increasingly taken to looking like that, except when on the stage in full public view, where he assumed a serious-but-happy facial expression. Gone was the naughty half smile and the twinkly eye. M was gazing into the zombie-eyes of a Waltertron.

"About your music," Charlie started. "It is of course very good, I like it very much, and it has its... erm... place".

M felt there was a 'but' coming.

"It is only that... erm... when you're leading the actual worship music... all that energy that you have... if you could put it into the... the mainstream worship style. If you could harmonise your style with that of Willie Booth, to ensure a unity of worship style across the services".

M looked at Charlie, but couldn't connect with him. This wasn't Charlie's words. It wasn't even his phraseology. It sounded like a government policy document, but M knew this was Walter's lines. A little incident came back to M and made sense. After Walter had first heard M sing he had later that day done something he had never done before or after: he had come into the reception area. He wore his aloof manners and proceeded to give M unasked for and unwanted advice on how to perform. *'Your gospel-imitation...'* was the only thing M could remember from what he had said. "Gospel-*imitation?*" What the hell was the guy on about? Did he think M stood on that stage and merely pretended? A Norwegian expression says that when you judge others you reveal *yourself*. Perhaps Walter was revealing how it was all an act for *him*. A lot of things would make sense if this was the case. Walter could not fathom how deeply M felt about the music. How he lost himself in it. How he was able to put his intellectualism to one side and simply be a child of God.

Rejoice in the Lord always: and again I say, Rejoice.
PHILIPPIANS IV; 4

Walter simply regarded him as another performer, like himself. After Charlie had gone M thought of a witty reply, 'oh I see, you want me to become a *franchise* worship leader?' But at the moment all he could manage was, 'I see'. It was appropriate enough. He did see. He saw Walter behind it. He saw the old Ice-Queen's hatred for real joy, for anyone claiming the limelight and admiration of the congregation other than him. The Ice-Queen demanded absolute subordination – no wonder so many talented people disappeared out of the Chelsea Chapel ministry after a while. The moment they started to shine the Ice-Queen subjected them to his frost. He had wanted to see M submitted. Perhaps he had hoped M would be so desperate to continue to sing that he would be willing to erase his own style and conform to the blandness of Willy Booth's style. For M this was never an option. Instead he wrote an email to Willy telling him to take him off the church song and worship roster. He would never sing at Chelsea Chapel again. It was another nail in the coffin. He knew he had to leave.

Having left his singing to one side M felt incomplete. But he also felt honest. Like a Howard Roark of gospel singing he had refused to compromise what he felt was *his* unique way of serving the Lord. He glided into a latter day mode. He now knew his days at Chelsea Chapel were numbered, but not yet the exact number. He passively went along with the G12-system. Jim had cleaned himself up. He came smartly dressed, groomed and prepared to contribute. M knew it was a far greater change than he could take credit for. Jim had had it in him and just needed a little friendly push. Daniel had grown in youthful confidence. He would've anyway, but M was glad if he had contributed in any little way. Jack was still unbearable to M, but at least he seemed to have stopped meddling.

With The Reader's Permission; A Digression

During services M took to wandering about the church. His excuse was that it was his duty to make sure everything was in order and functioning properly. The real reason was that he could no longer stand being in the service. At one such perambulation he ran into Helga, a lady he knew from the Bible Institute, hurrying back from a necessary errand. She admonished him for not being in the service, he made some jokey remark, but afterwards felt sad and empty. Helga was an Austrian lady, deep in middle age in terms of looks, attitudes *and* years. She was smallish, stooped slightly, wore square, steel-rimmed glasses, her hair was cut in a short, masculine fashion, the grey untouched by dye, and her plain looks unadorned by make-up. Her clothes were simply garments. They had the timelessness that meant they would be unstylish in all periods: a plain blouse, a dark pleated skirt (always skirts, never trousers), a beige raincoat and very sensible shoes (acquired through the National Health Service as they had to be especially made to her feet due to a condition of some sort). Helga had worked as a nurse for many years and carried the imprint of that calling in an over-earnest humourlessness of demeanour. On her face was the expression of the terminally harangued, only modified by a certain twinkle in the eye. She carried the guilt of someone who felt it their duty to always do more, no matter how much they are doing. Somewhere, someone was suffering due to *her* lack of omnipresence. And even as she came to the Bible College to learn how to be a more efficient servant of the Lord, she couldn't help thinking of all the people she could have helped and the hungry children that might've been fed using the money for the school fee, kindly paid by her home church in Austria.

Little grey Helga, with her grey eyes and greying hair, shuffling about in her NHS shoes not being noticed (except in the absence from any of her many duties). In her small home church she was a pillar, an essential building block. But in the huge Chelsea Chapel, London Metropolitan Church, it had been difficult for her to establish herself in a line of duty that made her indispensable, and this frustrated her. She would arrive early in the morning, walking quickly in small steps, hurrying so as not to disappoint someone by wasting time, although no one was waiting. Once there, she would help with something; carrying the tea urn, move some plants, setting up the lectern, the overhead projector, tidy something, anything. When M first saw her he *did* notice her. Immediately he despised her a little. It wasn't an emotion he articulated, even to himself – it was simply seeping into the stream of perception, polluting it, and making it impossible for M to take Helga quite seriously.

The suppressed sentiment expressed itself in a kind of congenial banter. Helga had a strong Austrian accent, so M would greet her everyday in mock Teutonic, "Ze hills are alive, wiz ze zound of Helga, yah?"

To which she would reply with just the flicker of a smile: "You are a *ferry* naughty boy M".

Yet M's almost compulsive levity in her presence had a deeper source. Helga might make some serious point about theology, or make a comment about a speaker, and M would respond with a joke.

"You must be more serious," she would admonish him ploddingly, and he would reply "jawohl!"

He was in fact trying to break a curse. M had realised, at a sub-conscious level at least, that Helga was not only right in her general attitude, but that she was a far more proper Christian than he was. She was *self-less* to the point of immolation, whilst M was rather full of himself. He saw himself as talented, intelligent, of superior taste and judgment. He found it nigh on impossible to defer to anyone unless they had, in his view, deserved his respect. It was one of the reasons he could never have even considered to become a nurse or doctor. To be constantly preoccupied with other people's suffering, to listen to their whinging and whining filled him with a sense of disgust. He had worked for a year at an old people's home. The building had three departments: the first floor was for short term patients; this was no fun as the inmates were not there long enough to get to know them. The second floor was for those needing permanent care, and this was the worst floor because the patient there were fully cognizant of their fate. Often bitter and sad, with memories of happier times and broken dreams they looked sullen and defeated. The third floor was for what they still called *senile dementia* patients. M had enjoyed this floor the best. This floor's crowd had gone beyond knowing about their suffering. They could still talk about the olden days that were seared unto their faltering brains, some of them could recite poems and sing hymns that they had learned when young. Some had gone beyond being able to speak. One old girl, thin as a stick and totally toothless, M fed breakfast every morning. Unlike the regular carers with their spreadsheets and economy, M took his time. He put lashings of butter and sugar on the porridge and fed her, looking at the fat dripping down her scrawny chin. She made yummy sounds, and M was happy in the knowledge that *he* had caused a little happiness in this old, miserable life. One morning she had, unprecedently, opened her eyes, turned her face towards M, fixed him with her pale eyes and exclaimed, "My, aren't you handsome!"

"And so are you" he replied.

"You think so?"

"Certainly".

She reshut her eyes and turned her face forward again, smiling contentedly.

And indeed, to him there was something beautiful in a human being experiencing a moment of guiltless pleasure. He could not imagine this being a source of beauty for Helga. For her, merely the word 'pleasure' would carry a tint of sin. She might accept the concept of 'deep happiness'; the state of knowing you had struggled as best you can – but never enough, never adequate. Helga had reminded M of a type of Christian he had never liked, but previously been able to wave off with Sigmund's guiltless theology. But the cracks in Sigmund's theology was becoming too obvious to him. The lacmus test for the soundness of Sigmund's teaching was that it would create a revival that the stagnated established churches had not been able to. But Sigmund had not seen any great revival, or even real growth. The peculiar brand of Christianity practiced at Happy Life Church had not been sustainable. People had either fallen off or almost imperceptibly changed their practice of faith by degrees towards a more mainstream understanding of Christian living, M and Sigmund included. And therefore, M could no longer assume that he and Sigmund were right and everybody else wrong. He had to face the fact that he and Sigmund were most probably wrong, and people like Helga right. It was Helga's Christianity that was Christianity. And M didn't want that Christianity.

For when the Gentiles, which have not the law, do by nature the
things contained in the law, these, having not the law,
are a law unto themselves
ROMANS II; 11 - 14

CHAPTER XVII

In which Pete acts in a strange way and our hero makes another decision

Pete's behaviour had become increasingly erratic. He disliked being pushed down the pecking order by his having to report to Charlie, rather than directly to Walter. He also disliked being eased out of personnel management, especially as it was Walter's wife – no HR professional – who took it over. After Sara Bruhn had left the media division there was no one left to delegate that work to until they found a replacement, but Pete knew it too was slipping through his fingers. He understood this from the fact that Charlie had started having meetings with those in the media department who hitherto had reported directly to Pete. And he particularly disliked having no actual office of his own. After the church moved its admin headquarters to a new open-plan office building, Pete and the Operations gang were on the ground floor, whilst the Senior Minister and Finance Department took the first floor, and had partitions built to create private offices for Walter, his wife and Charlie. Pete resented it deeply. He was still, though, the only one with the knowhow of how to deal with the management of the church's many big events. He was still the only go-to man when Walter wanted to hire Wembley Arena or the Royal Albert Hall. But whereas previously Walter had spoken directly to

Pete, he now posed all his questions to Charlie, who in turn put the questions to Pete, who answered Charlie who then told Walter. And if Walter had a follow-up question the process repeated itself. And because Charlie wanted to look prepared and avoid this, he started demanding lengthy memos from Pete answering every conceivable and unconceivable question in advance. M became caught up in this pantomime management process. Walter had expressed to Charlie his concern for the state of the carpet (full of chewing gum), the workings of the heating system (erratic at times) and the condition of the toilets (smelly). Charlie then in turn expressed this as his concerns to Pete, who then called M over to his desk (they only sat three metres apart) to let him know.

As M pulled up a chair, Pete sat with his head in his hands.

"Hi Pete, you okay?"

"I'll be alright presently. I've a blistering headache. Took a pill. M, could you be a lifesaver and make me a cup of tea. Strong enough for…

"… the spoon to stand up in it, yes I know. Will do".

Pete's PA had resigned, and Pete was no longer in a position to hire who he wanted. It was Walter's wife who led the process of recruiting, and who would interview and decide who would become Pete's PA. Pete hated that too.

"Charles is sending me so many memos, I am sure he is killing off a rainforest every week," Pete said with an exasperated look on his face. He lifted up a pile of papers.

"I mean, he wants to know the ins and the outs of a duck's arse!"

M chuckled. "Yes, I guess he is trying to appear prepared to Walter".

"Well, on the issue of Walter… He's been traipsing about the church looking into every crook and granny to find something to complain about. Here…" He handed the memo from Bruce over to M.

It was written in a curt and sourly tone.

But although he wanted, in loyalty, to sympathize with Pete, a part of M felt it was perfectly reasonable for the senior leader to raise these issues, and that Pete had somewhat failed in not noticing first that there were issues. Perhaps his mind had been otherwise occupied.

"On the toilets...that is easy enough, I will speak to the caretakers and put in place a system where they sign off every time they clean it. But the heating system is very old and needs a general servicing and possibly some repair, and on the state of the carpet... what I suggest, Pete, is that we reply telling them that that old carpet will never look good. We need to change the floor covering. Being a Scandinavian I would suggest wooden flooring, or some such material that is easy to clean".

Pete leaned back in his chair and held his arms out apologetically.

"M, if I were the one who pulled the strings we'd do all that you say, but they're treating me like a schoolboy." He leaned forward, "but write the memo with the points you mentioned. At least we can cover our backs by having it in writing".

He sipped his tea and looked sad.

In the ensuing days M was on the floor with the caretakers on all fours scraping chewing gum off the carpets, deep cleaning the toilets, and looking at the boiler with an engineer, to see what might be done. Pete spoke on his mobile phone. Pete had always spent a lot of time on his mobile, but lately the thing had seemed glued to his ear. He had a worried look on his face, which he tried to dispel when he saw M; with a smile so forced it only had the effect of drawing attention to the fact that a *forced* smile was necessary. Over a cup of coffee he told M that he had been instructed to vacate the flat he'd had at the church's townhouse property. Now he had rented a bedsit, but it wasn't satisfactory. M had a brainwave and suggested he move in with him. Since M had taken Arthur Kentworthy's house he'd shared with a fellow Bible Institute student, but he had left and so he now had an empty spare bedroom and a tight economy. If he could share the rent... Pete hesitated, but came around to the idea.

M had thought, perhaps naively, that in sharing digs Pete would feel better for the odd couple comradery. The two of them – the common sense folks – against the flaky leadership. But every day Pete left very early and came home very late. The weekends were spent out of London, presumably at his country house, M thought, but couldn't help suspecting something else. Occasionally – when M happened to be still awake – Pete staggered out of his car, visibly drunk as he entered the house. He seemed increasingly pensive, harried and unresponsive.

Where before, when M had suggested something, he would say, 'do it', he now invariably held up his chubby, hairy arms – always clad in a short-sleeved shirt – and expressed regret at his powerlessness. M found him more and more pathetic.

Then M had a phone call:

"Hello is that Mr M -----?

"Yes, that's me"

"Oh good morning, my name is Mr Davies, I am from the rental agency who deals with Mr Kentworthy's house"

"Oh yes, I remember you, when we drew up the new contract with Mr Pete Crawley.

"Precisely. That is what I am calling about. I'm, afraid Mr Crawley has not been paying any rent for his share of the house, and under the terms and conditions that makes the other party – you in other words – liable for his share of the rent."

"Oh really?"

"Yes, I'm afraid so. Are you able to speak to Mr Crawley to see if he might be able to pay up?"

"Yes, yes of course, I do see him regularly so... I will mention it."

"Thank you, that would be good I think. As I said, you have a certain interest in making sure Mr Crawley pays his share."

M hung up and felt dizzy. When he spoke to Pete about it he angrily denied there was a problem, and said he had already spoken to them and that they had no business calling M about it. But M knew he was lying, and that it was quite correct of the agency to involve him as a liable party. It was strange, erratic behaviour. Pete's change from proactive bull in charge, to a passive, rejected circus-bear; his constantly being on the phone; his not spotting the things that needed doing – something he used to, his mental absence at times; it all came together and meant something. But what exactly? M thought of the job-offer Pete had had previously. Perhaps he was already working for someone else, and biding his time to jump ship. Then he disappeared.

After a few days of uncertainty M was informed by Charlie that Pete would be off sick for a while. M felt slightly hurt that Pete had not confided in him. Normally M would have been excited by the opportunity such a situation created. But now he mostly felt exposed, not having Pete to buffer between him and Charlie. At the same time he felt a certain responsibility. He had wanted to resign, but how could he now? In a meeting with Joe Williams, the finance director of the church – a pedantic accountant with a childish excitement for Excel spreadsheets and a servile loyalty to Walter – M had a surprise. Williams had always felt he had some special affinity to M based on his being married to a Scandinavian. He now leaned forward with a conspiratorial smile.

"You know M," he said, "Walter has his eye on you to take over from Pete".

M did not know what to say to this. He had not felt he was in any way the flavour of the month. Still, he supposed they didn't have anyone else. Well, he was determined they wouldn't have him either. Not very much longer. But he was somewhat satisfied that they had realised they needed him. That they thought he was good enough to take over from Pete. It was almost enough to consider to stay. But although M enjoyed his work, if not the leadership, there was a deeper problem: his faith had changed. He no longer believed that the sort of Christianity preached, and sometimes practiced, at Chelsea Chapel was the kind he wanted to see. The impossible belief in miraculous healings and the power of prayer to change reality; he had seen it fail too many times; he had seen those anointed and chosen by God misbehave and fail too many times; he had seen too many examples of behaviour impossible if people really were filled with The Holy Ghost, his own failings included.

There were only two alternatives left: either the power of God is very weak and the Holy Ghost makes no difference to people's lives, or the whole theology is wrong and the relationship between God and humankind is totally different from what he had believed so far. He thought the latter was the more probable. If there is a God his power will not be weak, but it might operate in a different way. A way that will make his experiences make sense. He wasn't sure what exactly he should believe, only that the teaching and practices of the established churches were a lot closer to what made sense than the teachings he had tried to follow for more than ten years. Around this time Willy Booth called and asked if M wanted to take over the choir. M thought it strange how these offers came now, as he was standing at the precipice ready to jump. Why not a year ago or two? Did they not realise how he felt about the church, about Walter and the whole G12-thing? No, it was impossible now.

It was approaching autumn. M realised this would be the fifth autumn at the Chelsea Chapel. How many services, meetings and conferences had he organised or taken part in? He'd worked at the Royal Albert Hall, Wembley Arena, Methodist Central Hall in Westminster, countless west-end hotels, Earls Court, and many other places across the capital.

And every day of every week he had made sure the place kept ticking over; ensured that toilet rolls were in supply, that the cleaning was done, that rooms were tidied and organised, broken down photocopiers mended, quotes obtained for work, stationery ordered, that the church looked spic and span, that the baptismal fount was filled, and all other jobs big and small that make up the running of a modern church in a modern world.

And he felt sad.

Sad, because he knew he could not continue. M loved his work. It had been the best of jobs and it had been the worst of jobs. The pace and intensity of it at times. The need to be highly organised. The management of staff, the buzz of services and big events. But he had become a mere observer. He never took part in the worship or the prayers, he didn't listen to the sermons – and if he did he could only think of how stupid and vacuous they sounded. His whole belief in that sort of Christianity had withered as he had matured. He had felt a sense of loyalty to Pete, but now he was gone, that was drying up as well.

Sigmund had left the Metropolitan Church Network long ago, and it was a long time since M had felt any loyalty for Walter or indeed for Charlie. In the beginning, M recalled, whenever Pete went for one of his walkabouts he could at first strike terror in the heart of the staff he ran into. But soon he'd be joking and chatting and leaving a trail of laughter and cheeky smiles. When Walter went for one of his, thankfully extremely seldom, walkabouts it was the Queen of Frost leaving a train of disheartened and dispirited church workers – some in floods of tears. If Walter entered a room conversation ceased, smiles dissipated and hitherto relaxed bodies went rigid. M warmly remembered the Sunday Walter was away and the previous pastor – the Welshman Will Davies – took his place for the day. The way he put M at ease with his little gestures of friendliness and show of trust. It inspired a feeling of worth and a desire to follow. Walter inspired nothing but spite in M. He didn't want to follow Walter. So he had to come to the final question: should he stay or should he go now? Had it been God calling him or simply London calling? He had been an anglophile all his life. His mother used to tell him how, as a six-year-old, M had looked at a calendar of English castles and said, "one day I will live there". Perhaps God's voice was simply his own. In which case he could leave Chelsea Chapel any time he wanted.

As he exited South Kensington tube station on his way to the church that morning, into the constant flow of people, he noticed the clear, blue skies. It was a nice, bright, late summer day in September, with only a hint of the coming autumn in the air. He walked fast going through a list of things in his head to check: had the broken photocopier been seen to? Had the quote on the roof work arrived? Had the caretakers cleaned the upstairs after last night's meeting?

The Chelsea Chapel building was normally a hive of activity, with people constantly running to and fro, telephones ringing, voices shouting, rehearsals going on. But as M entered there was an eerie silence. The receptionists were staring into a screen playing a news report. M went over. On the screen M saw in slow motion as an aeroplane silently crashed into a tall skyscraper. A ball of fire, the collapse. M stood transfixed. The silent church was all around him. The world felt dirty, unshaven, and full of unpleasant surprises. Things could only get worse.

And when he had opened the fourth seal, I heard the voice of the
fourth beast say, Come and see.
And I looked, and behold a pale horse: and his name that sat on
him was Death, and Hell followed with him.
And power was given unto them over the fourth part of the earth,
to kill with sword, and
with hunger, and with death, and with the beasts of the earth.
REVELATION VI; 6 – 8

And he said unto me, These sayings are faithful and true.
REVELATION XXII; 6

ND - #0208 - 270225 - C0 - 234/156/9 - PB - 9781780915326 - Gloss Lamination